HAYLEE AND COMET

A Trip Around the Sun

Roaring Brook Press
New York

To my brothers:
Jason, Josh, Justin, and Jordan,
who have walked beside me in this life,
bearing witness to all the change—
long enough to know that part of me
is still the same. —DM

Published by Roaring Brook Press
Roaring Brook Press is a division of Holtzbrinck Publishing Holdings Limited Partnership
120 Broadway, New York, NY 10271 • mackids.com

Library of Congress Control Number: 2021906546
ISBN 978-1-250-77440-8

Our books may be purchased in bulk for promotional, educational, or business use.
Please contact your local bookseller or the Macmillan Corporate and Premium Sales Department
at (800) 221-7945 ext. 5442 or by email at MacmillanSpecialMarkets@macmillan.com.

First edition, 2021 • Book design by Kirk Benshoff

The art for this book was rendered with ink, colored pencils, watercolor, gouache,
and acrylic paint on hot press watercolor paper.

Printed in China by Toppan Leefung Printing Ltd., Dongguan City, Guangdong Province

1 3 5 7 9 10 8 6 4 2

THE
COCOON

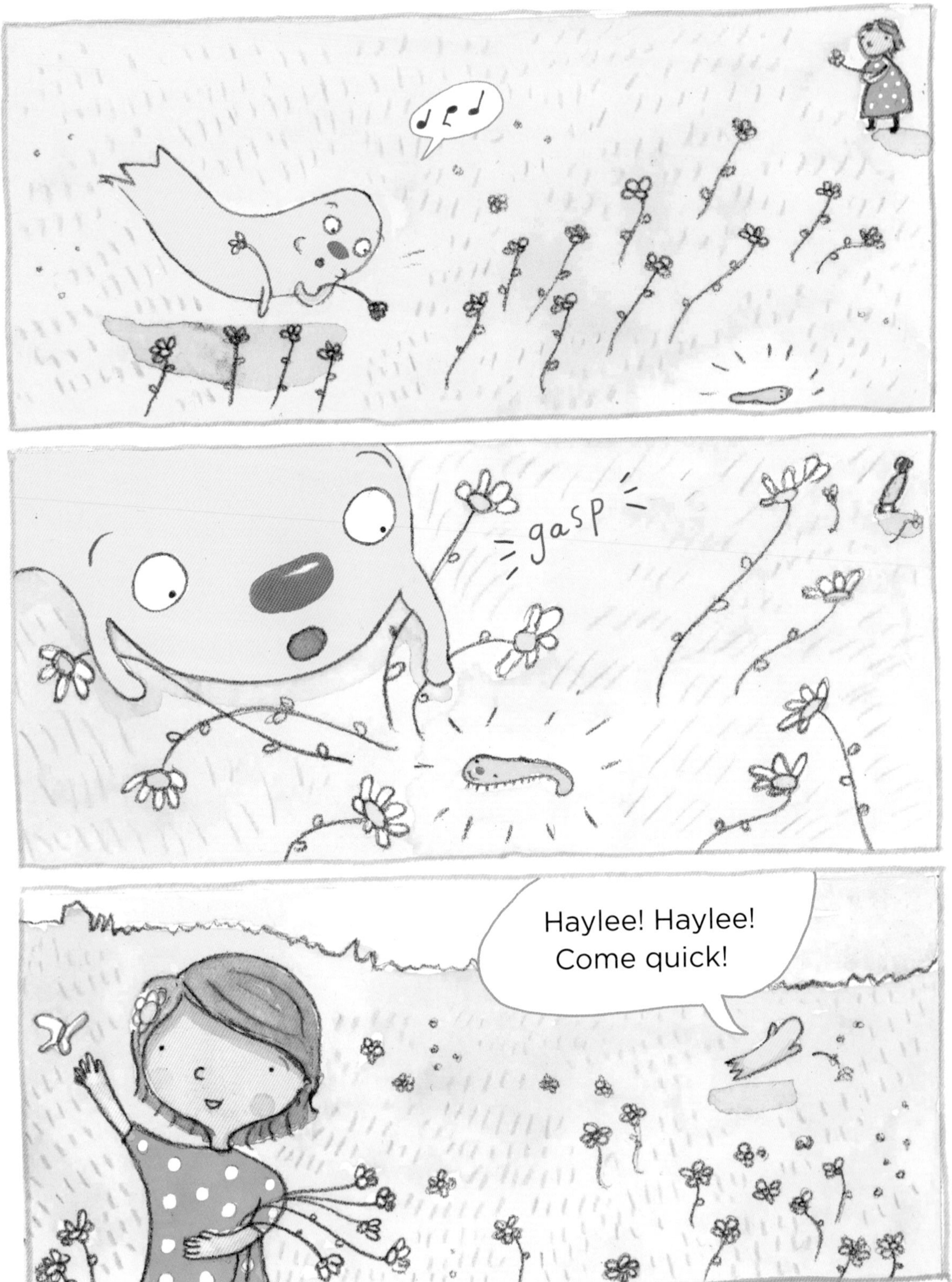
gasp
Haylee! Haylee!
Come quick!

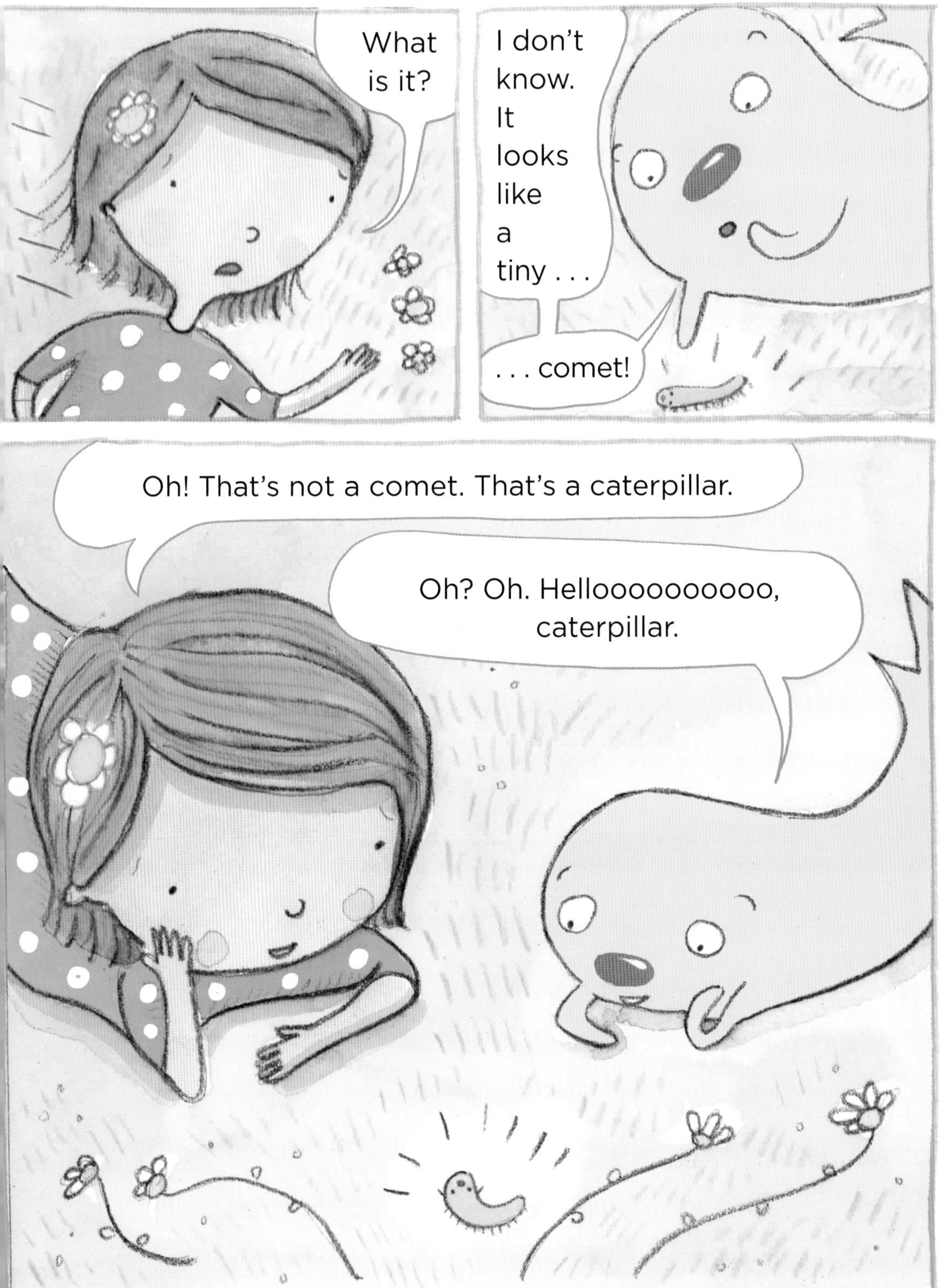
What is it?
I don't know. It looks like a tiny . . .
. . . comet!
Oh! That's not a comet. That's a caterpillar.
Oh? Oh. Hellooooooooooo, caterpillar.

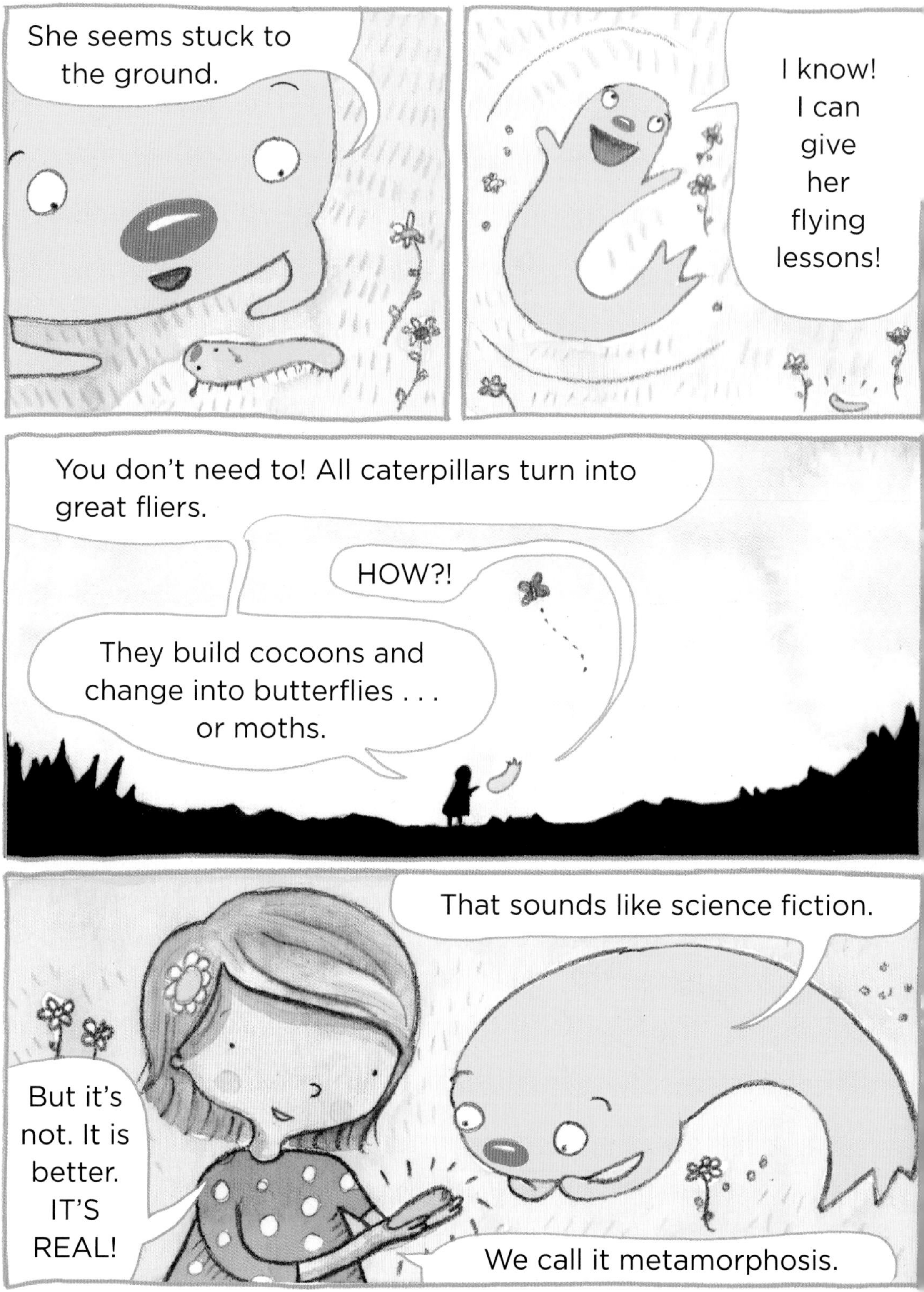
She seems stuck to the ground.
I know! I can give her flying lessons!
You don't need to! All caterpillars turn into great fliers.
HOW?!
They build cocoons and change into butterflies . . . or moths.
That sounds like science fiction.
But it's not. It is better. IT'S REAL!
We call it metamorphosis.

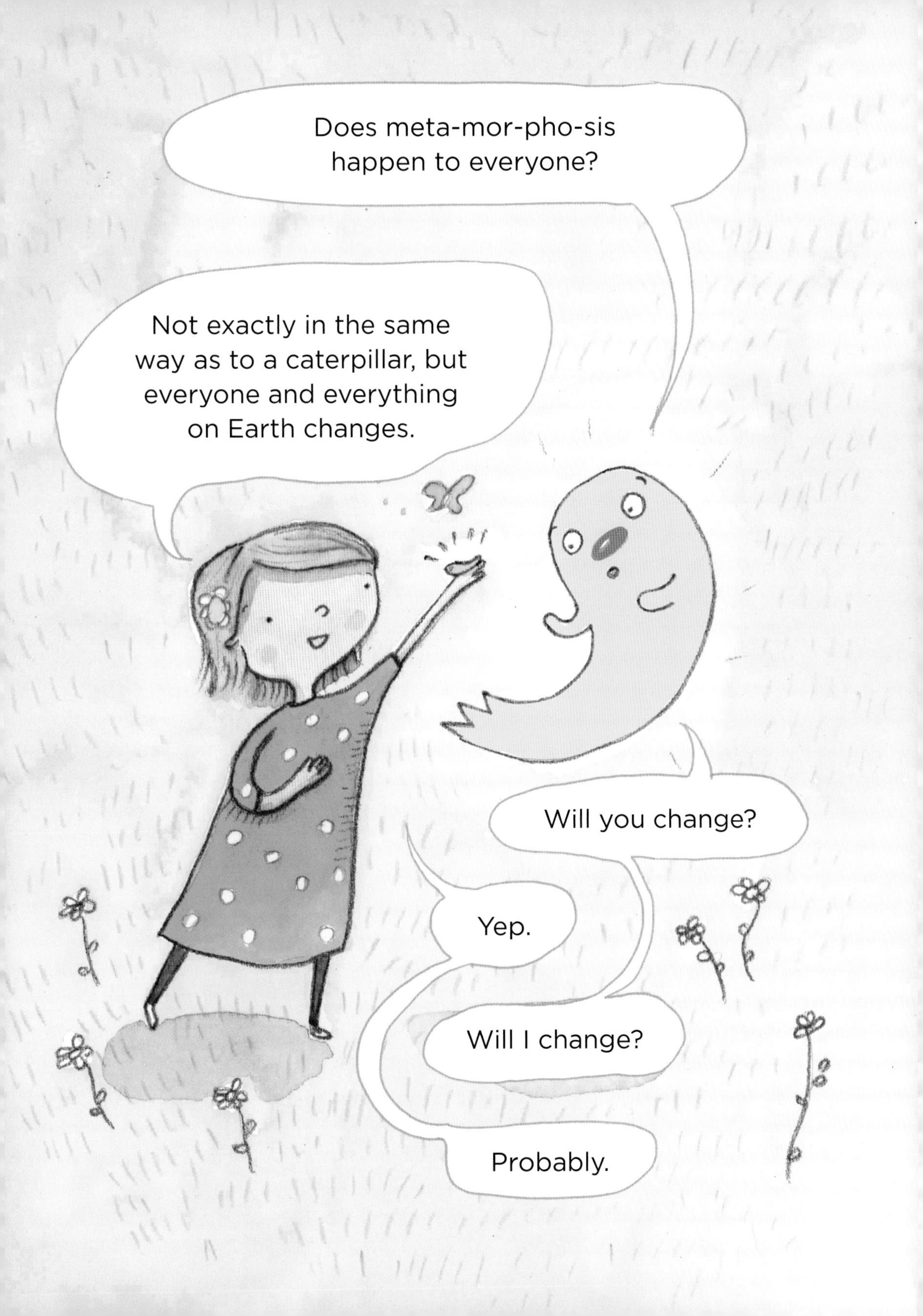
Does meta-mor-pho-sis happen to everyone?
Not exactly in the same way as to a caterpillar, but everyone and everything on Earth changes.
Will you change?
Yep.
Will I change?
Probably.

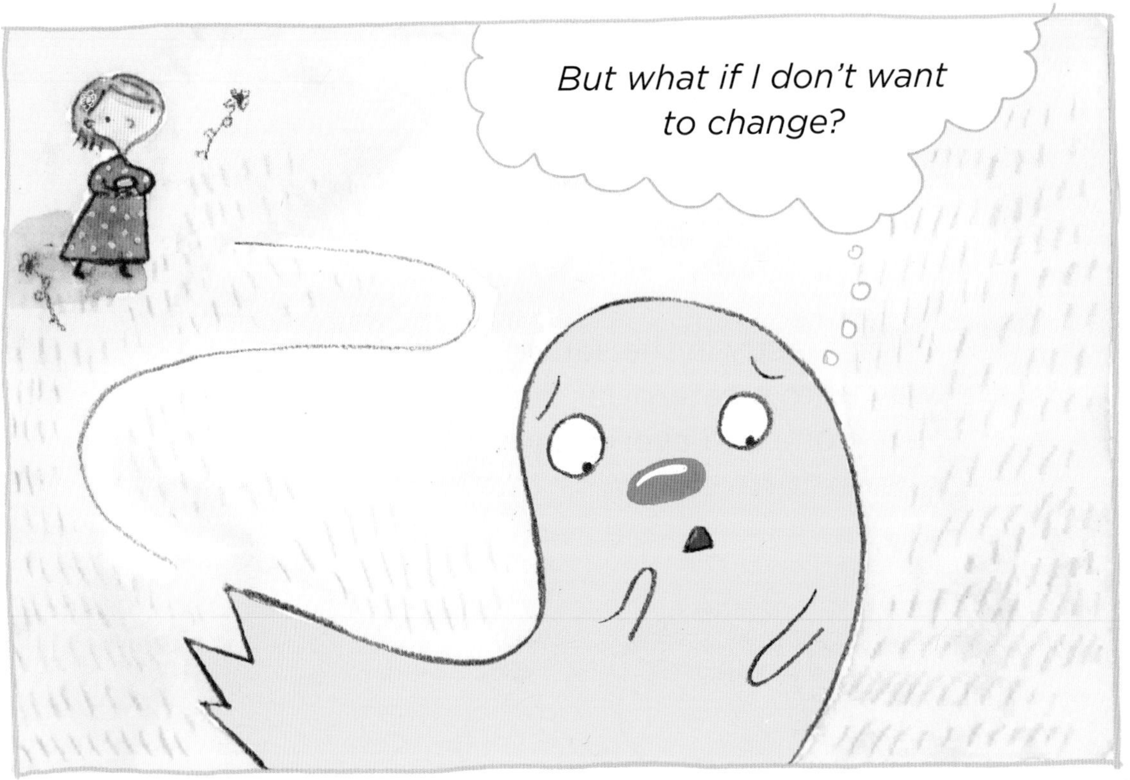
But what if I don't want to change?

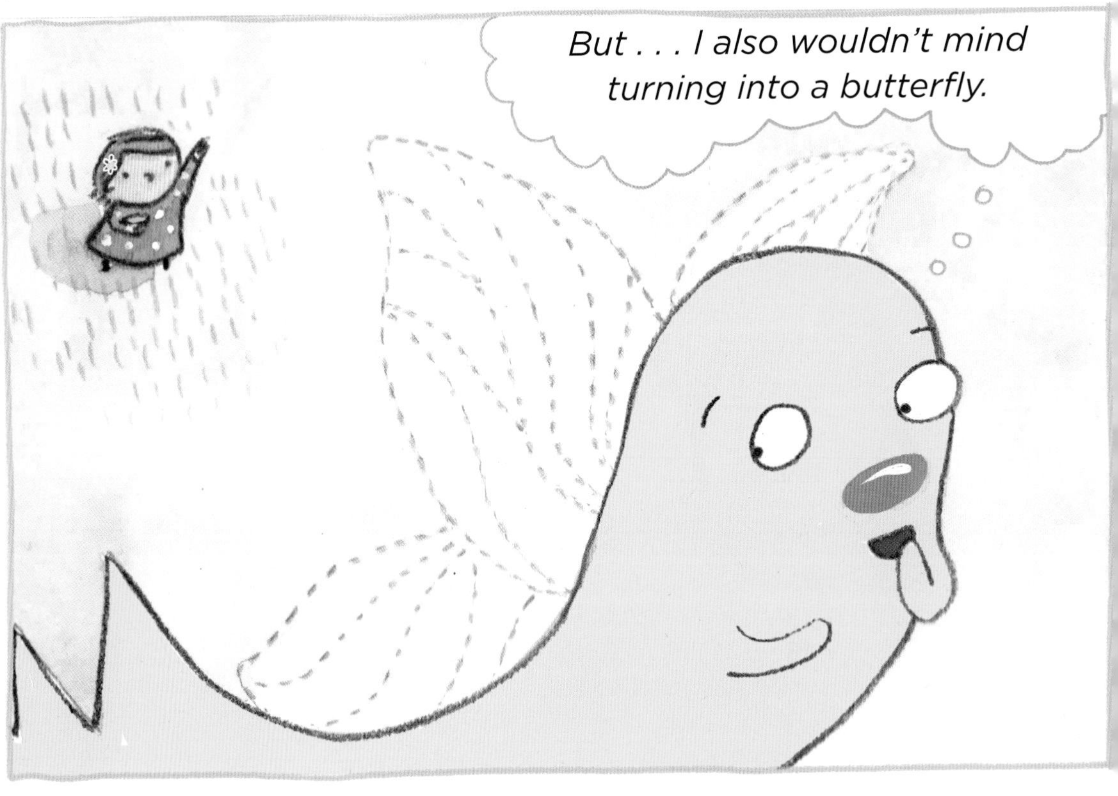
But . . . I also wouldn't mind turning into a butterfly.

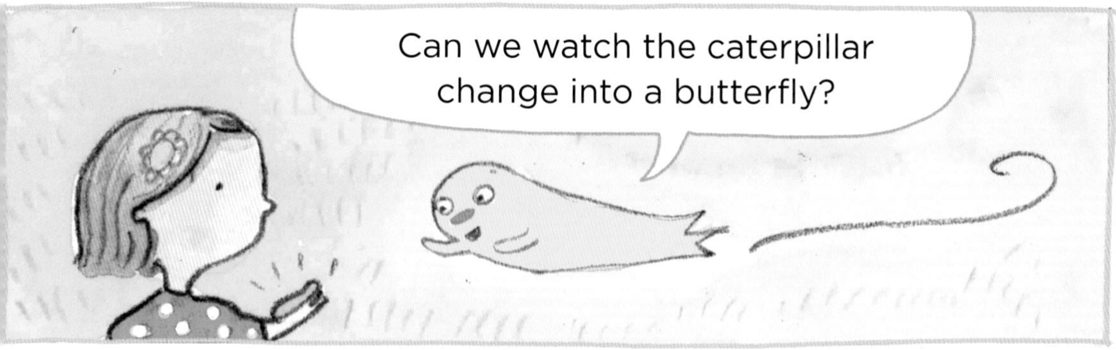
Can we watch the caterpillar change into a butterfly?

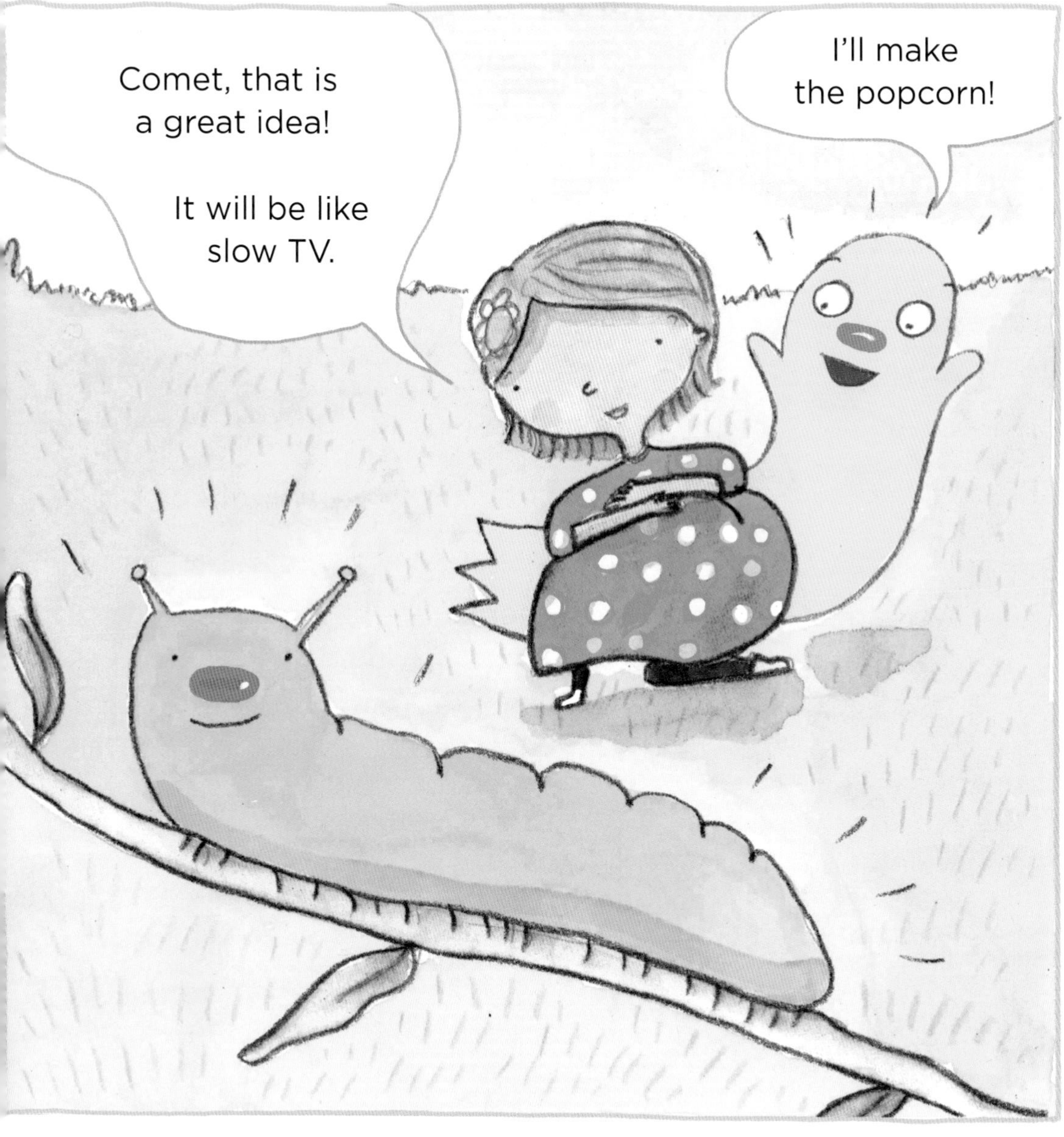
Comet, that is a great idea!
It will be like slow TV.
I'll make the popcorn!

Step 1.
Find a good spot.

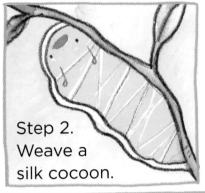

Step 2.
Weave a
silk cocoon.

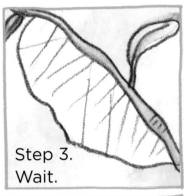

Step 3.
Wait.

I wonder if the caterpillar
is lonely in there.

We can let her know we're here.

Of
course!

Once upon
a time . . .

Twinkle, twinkle, little
star . . .

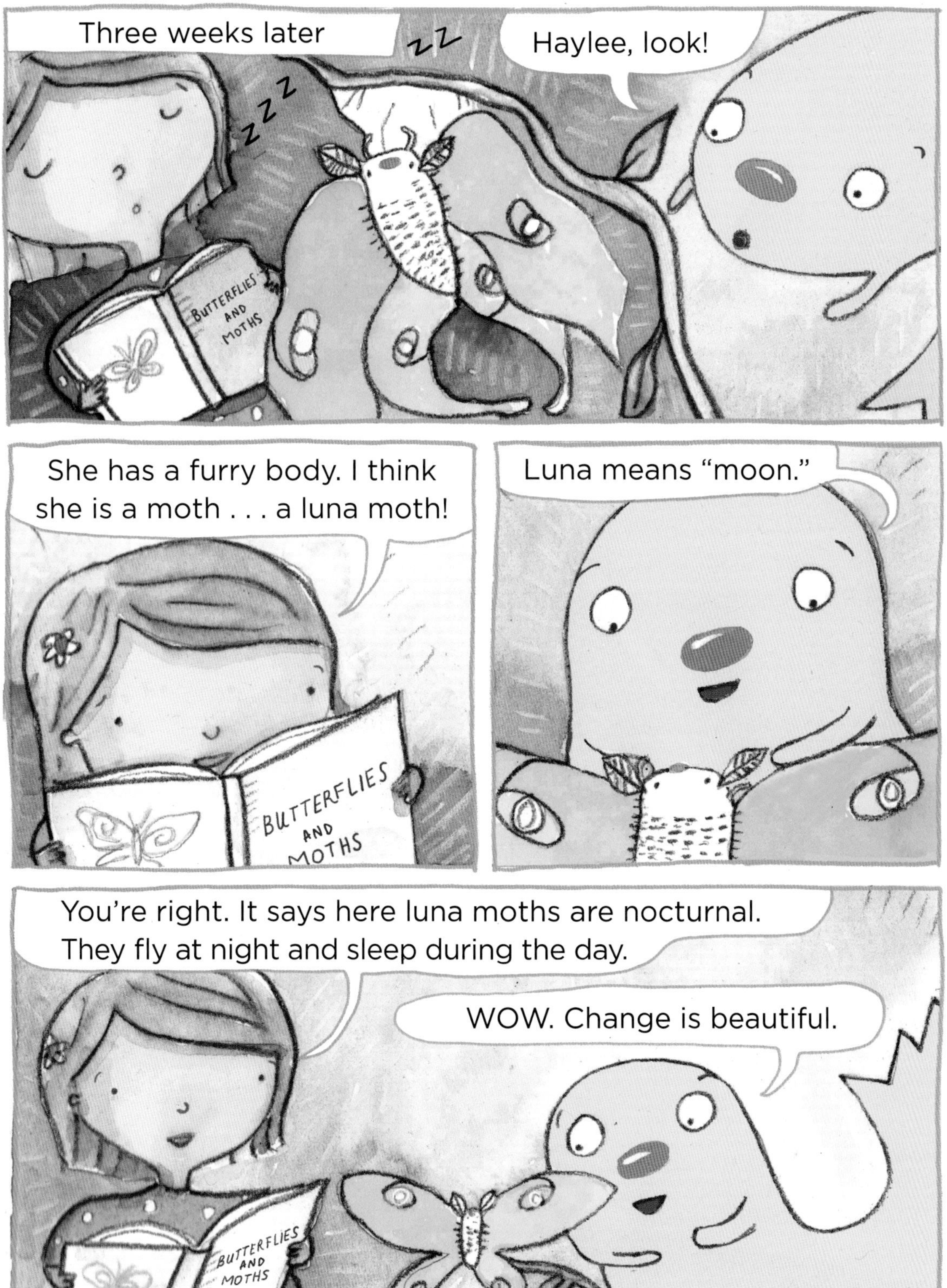
Three weeks later
ZZ
ZZZ
Haylee, look!
BUTTERFLIES AND MOTHS
She has a furry body. I think she is a moth . . . a luna moth!
BUTTERFLIES AND MOTHS
Luna means "moon."
You're right. It says here luna moths are nocturnal. They fly at night and sleep during the day.
WOW. Change is beautiful.
BUTTERFLIES AND MOTHS

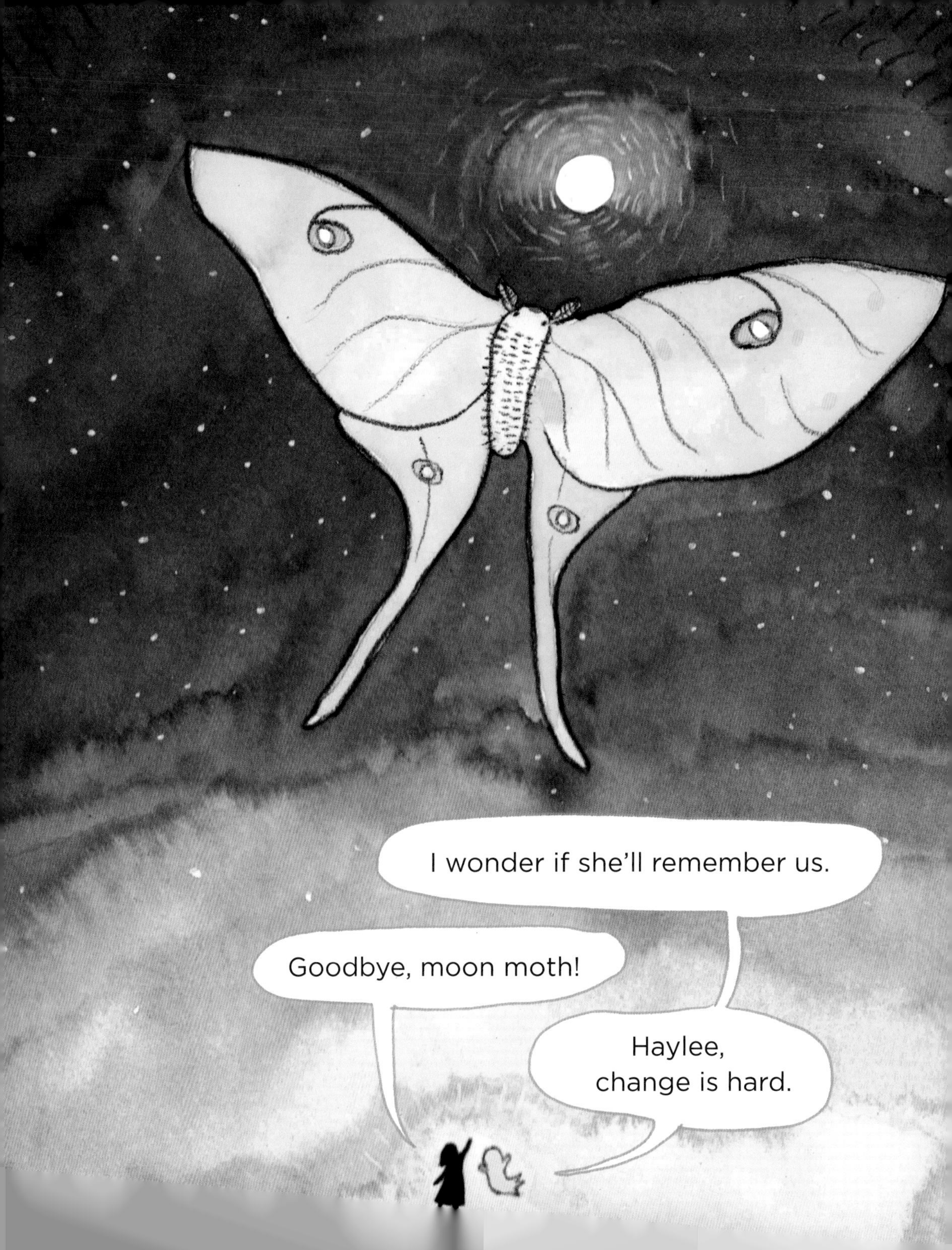
I wonder if she'll remember us.
Goodbye, moon moth!
Haylee,
change is hard.

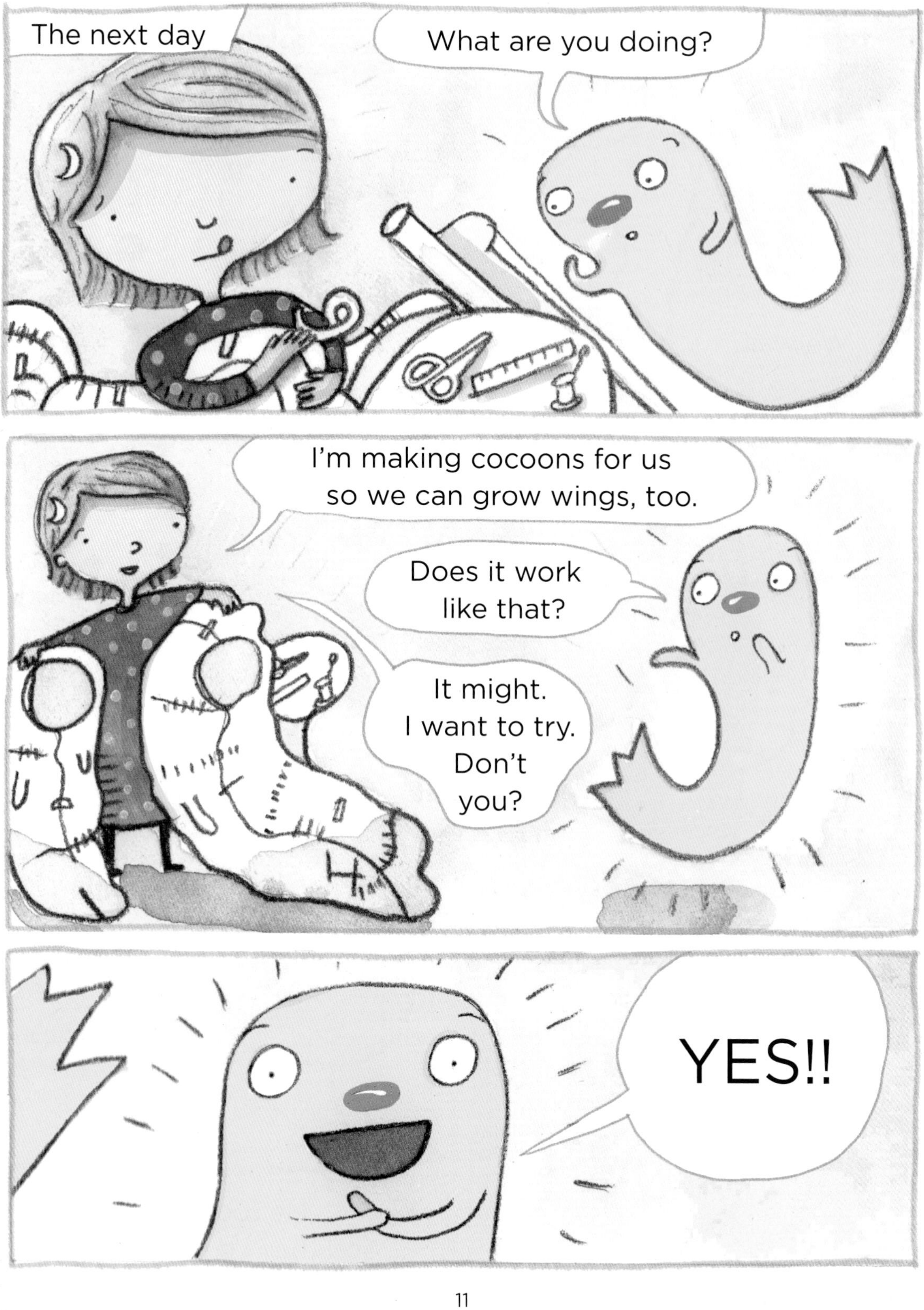
The next day
What are you doing?
I'm making cocoons for us so we can grow wings, too.
Does it work like that?
It might. I want to try. Don't you?
YES!!

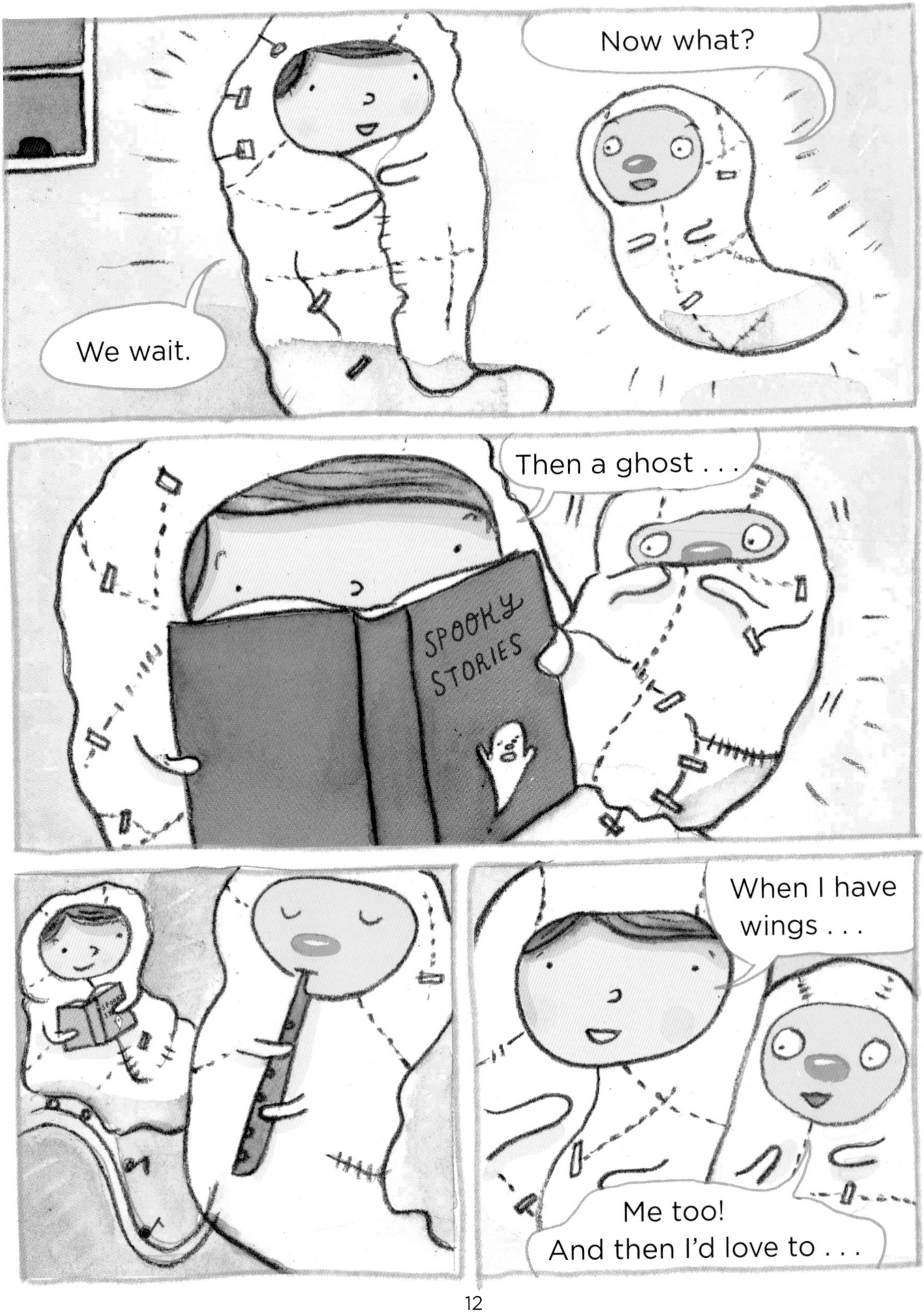
Now what?
We wait.
Then a ghost . . .
SPOOKY STORIES
When I have wings . . .
Me too! And then I'd love to . . .

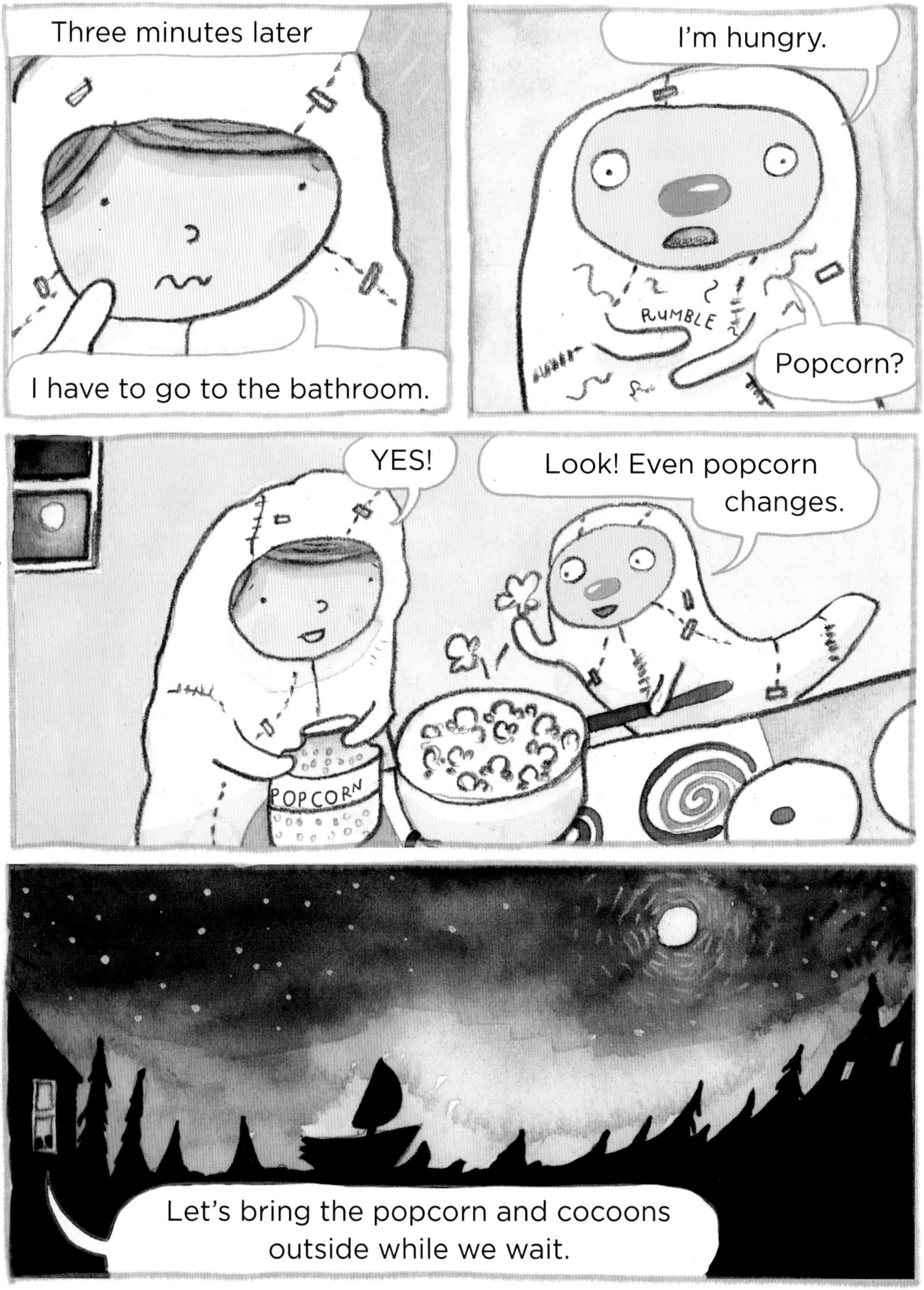
Three minutes later
I have to go to the bathroom.
I'm hungry.
RUMBLE
Popcorn?
YES!
Look! Even popcorn changes.
POPCORN
Let's bring the popcorn and cocoons outside while we wait.

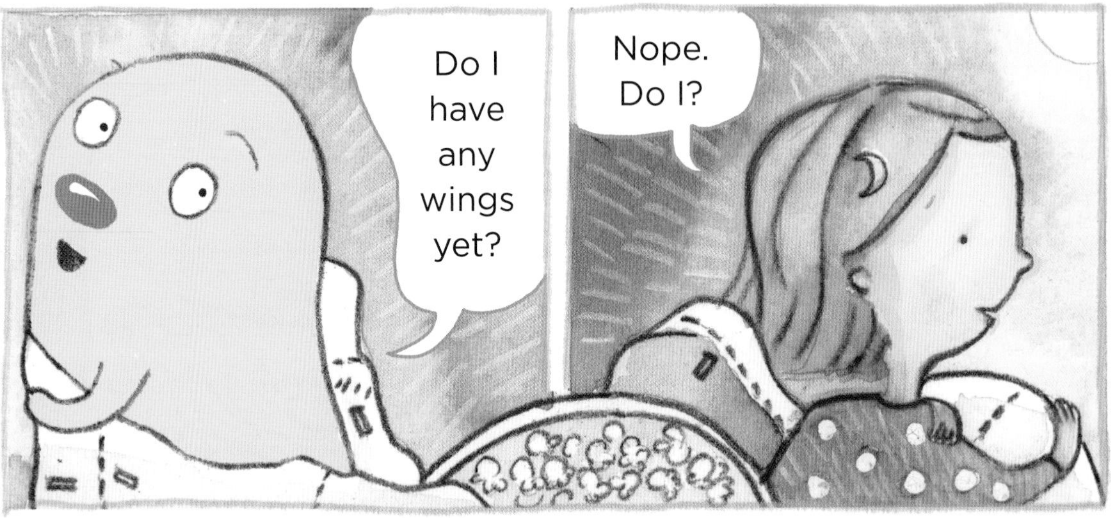
Do I have any wings yet?
Nope. Do I?

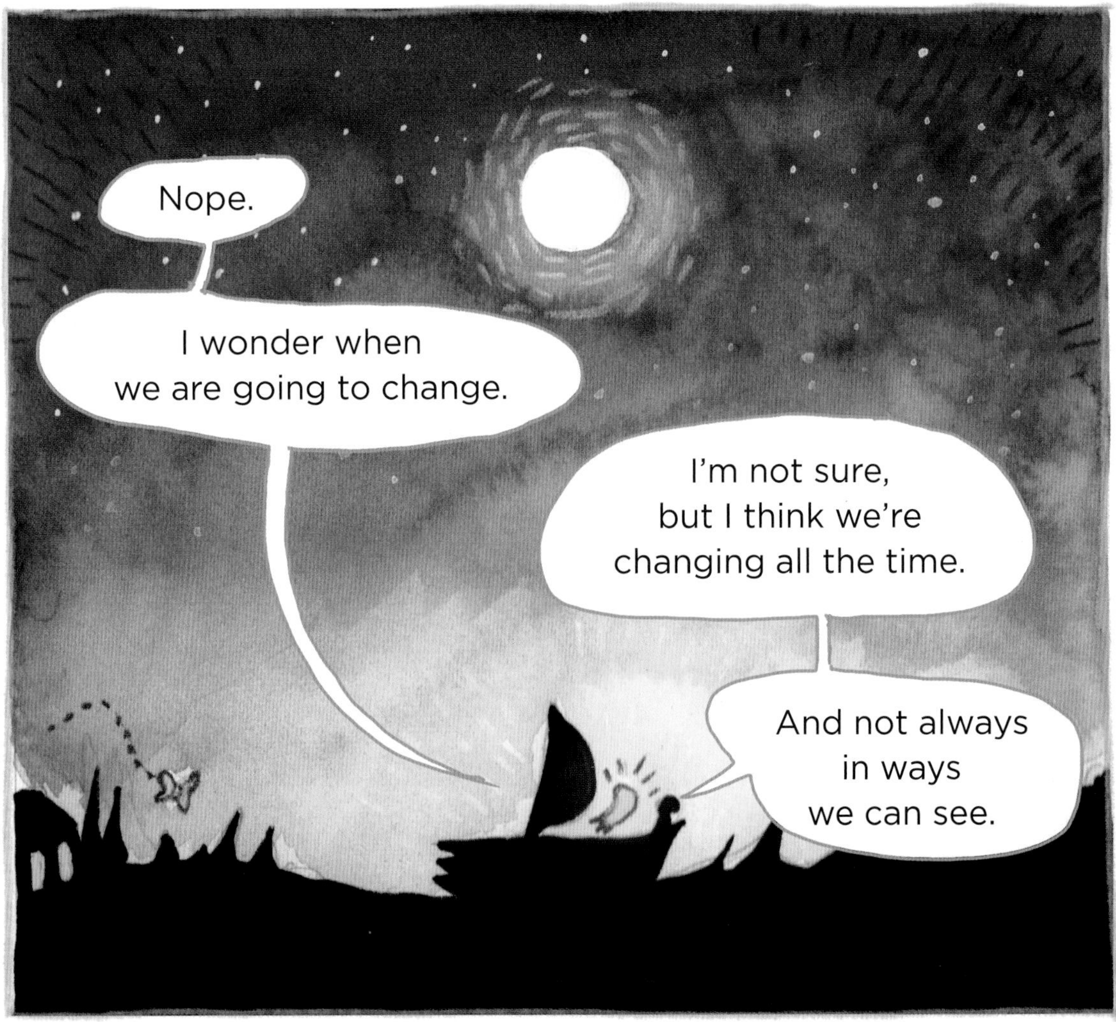
Nope.
I wonder when we are going to change.
I'm not sure, but I think we're changing all the time.
And not always in ways we can see.

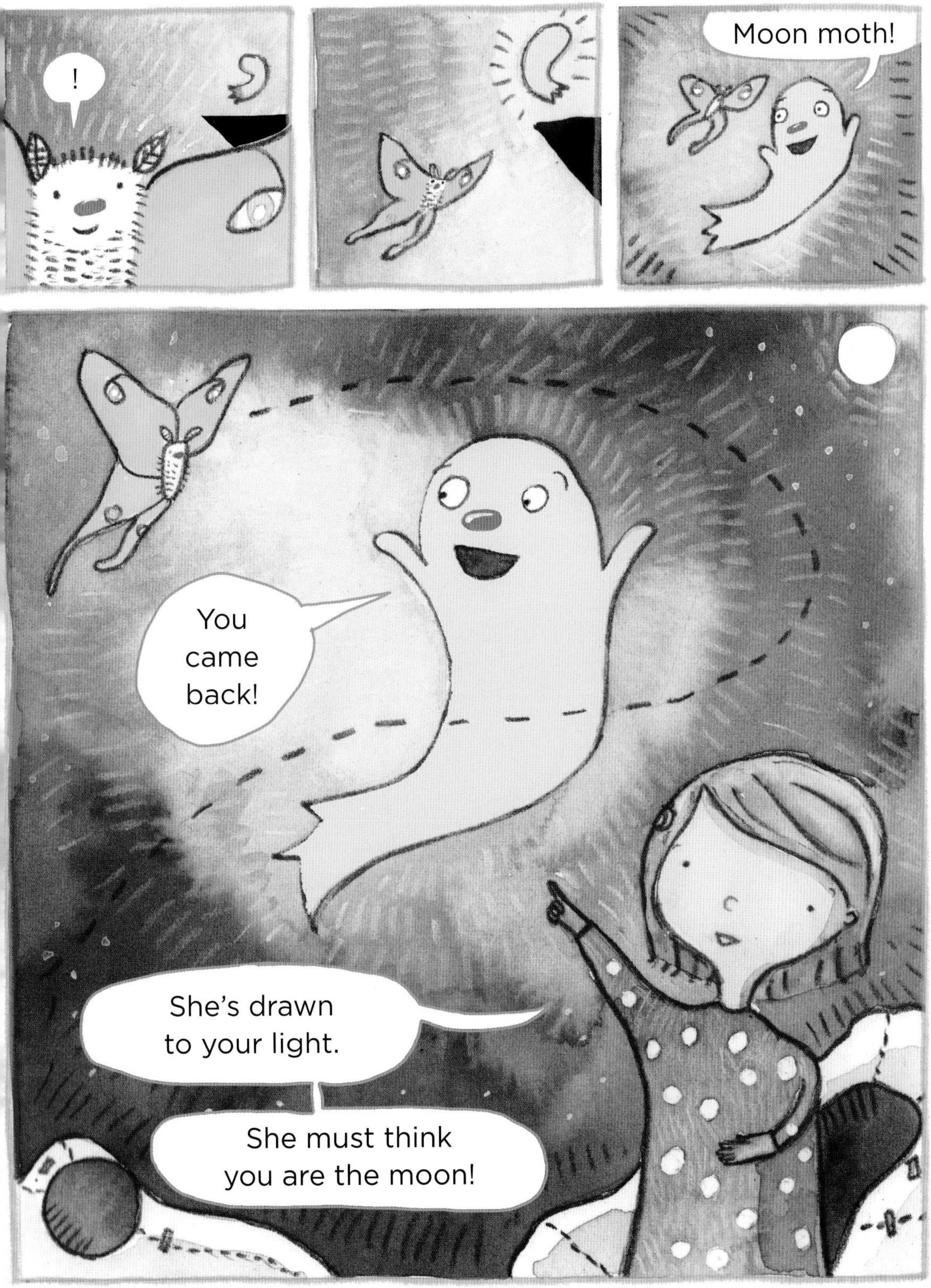
!
Moon moth!
You came back!
She's drawn to your light.
She must think you are the moon!

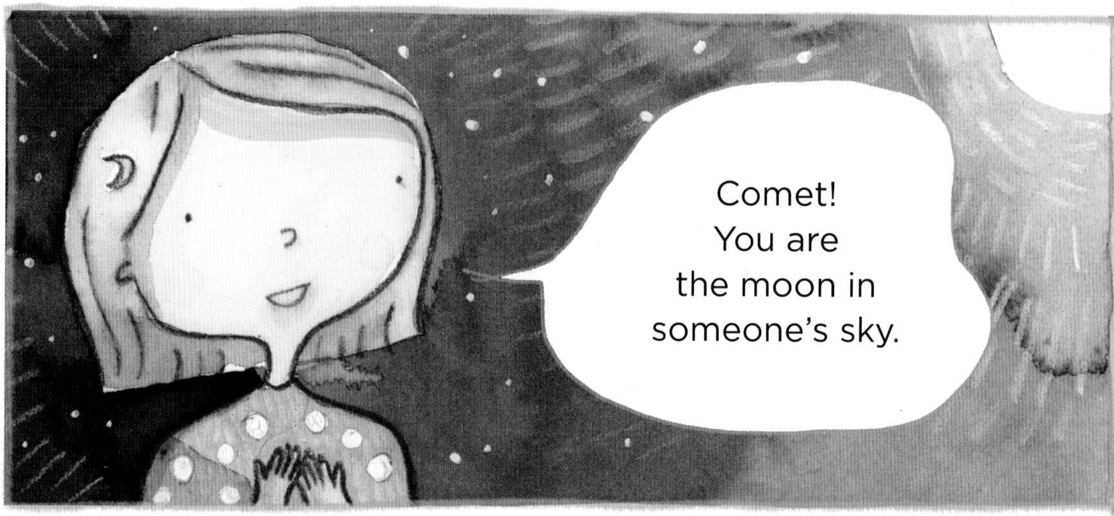
Comet!
You are
the moon in
someone's sky.

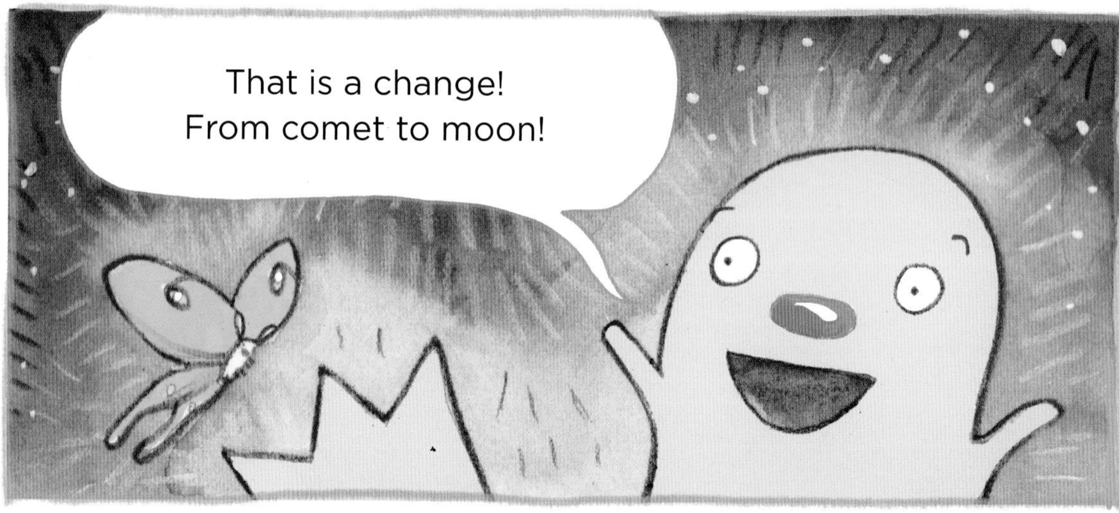
That is a change!
From comet to moon!

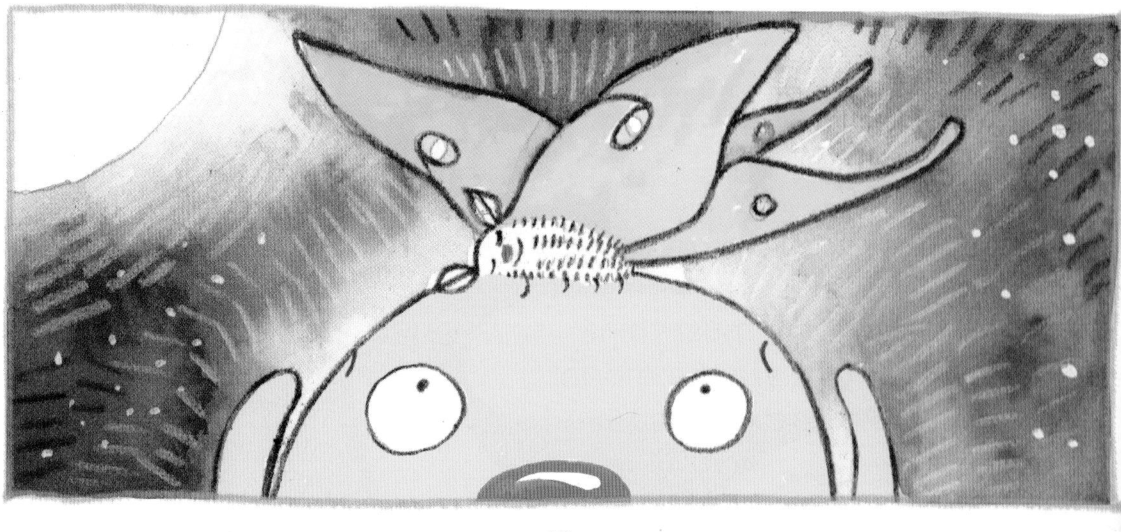

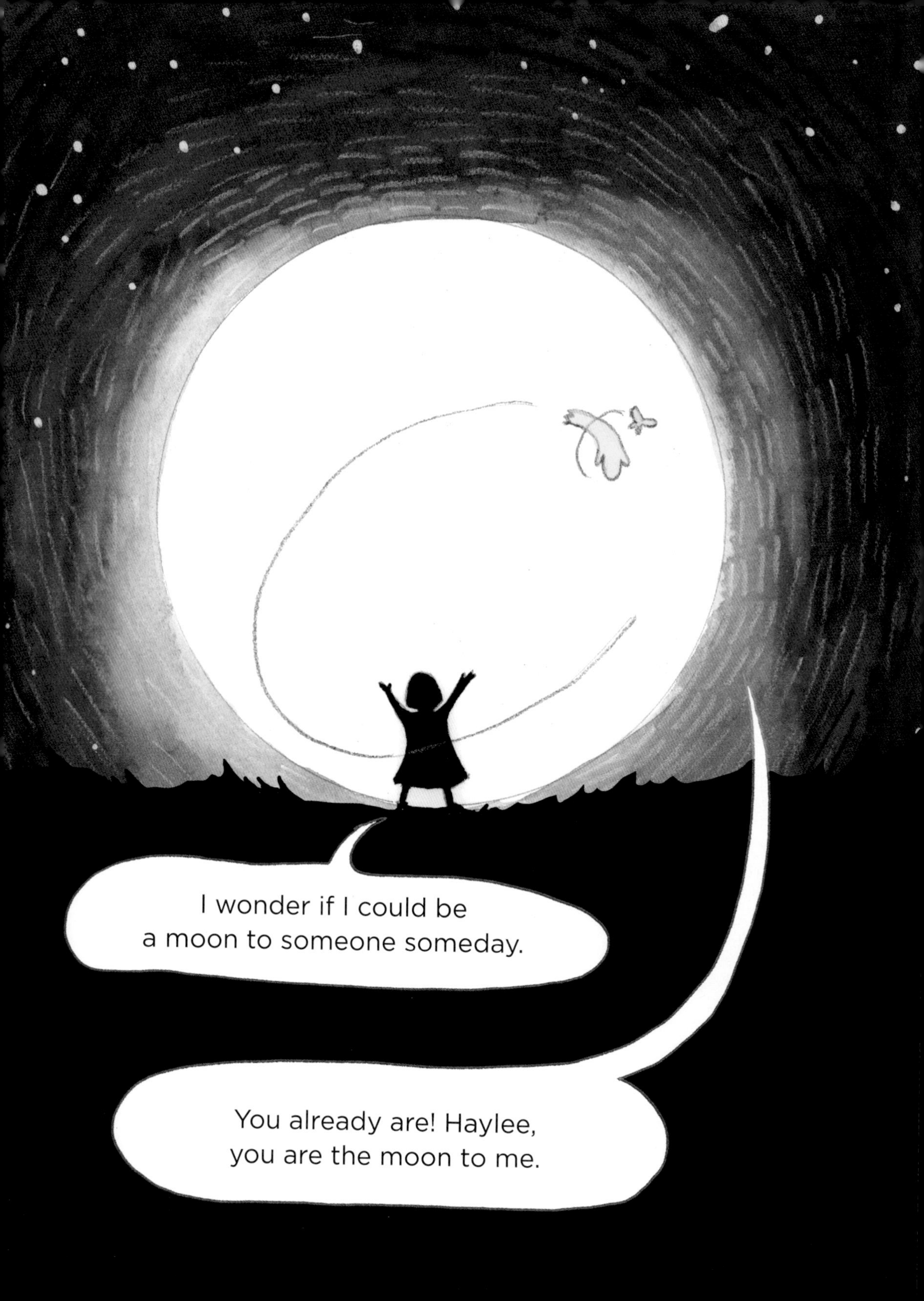
I wonder if I could be a moon to someone someday.
You already are! Haylee, you are the moon to me.

Why are moths drawn to light anyway?

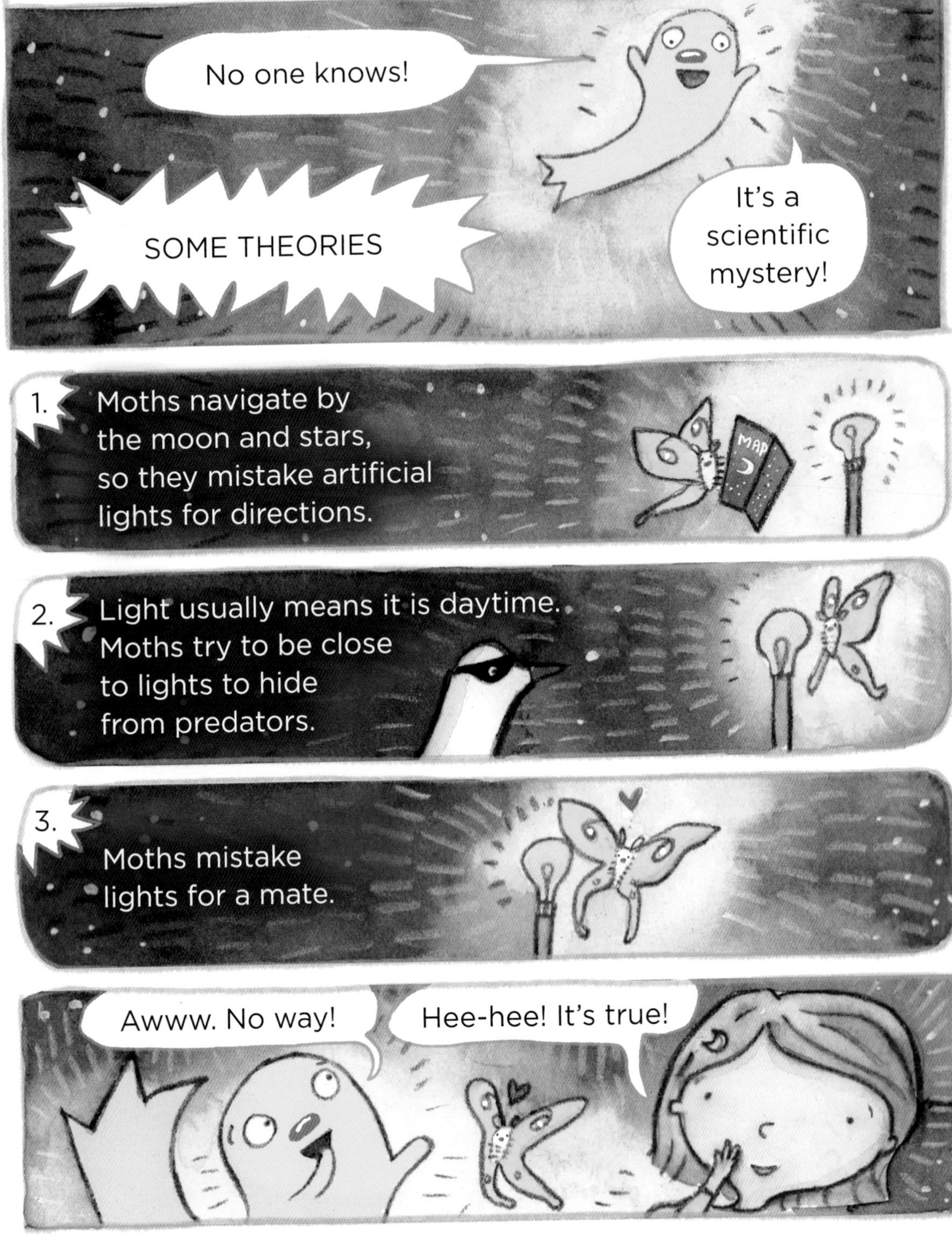
No one knows!
SOME THEORIES
It's a scientific mystery!
1. Moths navigate by the moon and stars, so they mistake artificial lights for directions.
MAP
2. Light usually means it is daytime. Moths try to be close to lights to hide from predators.
3. Moths mistake lights for a mate.
Awww. No way!
Hee-hee! It's true!

SNOW CONE

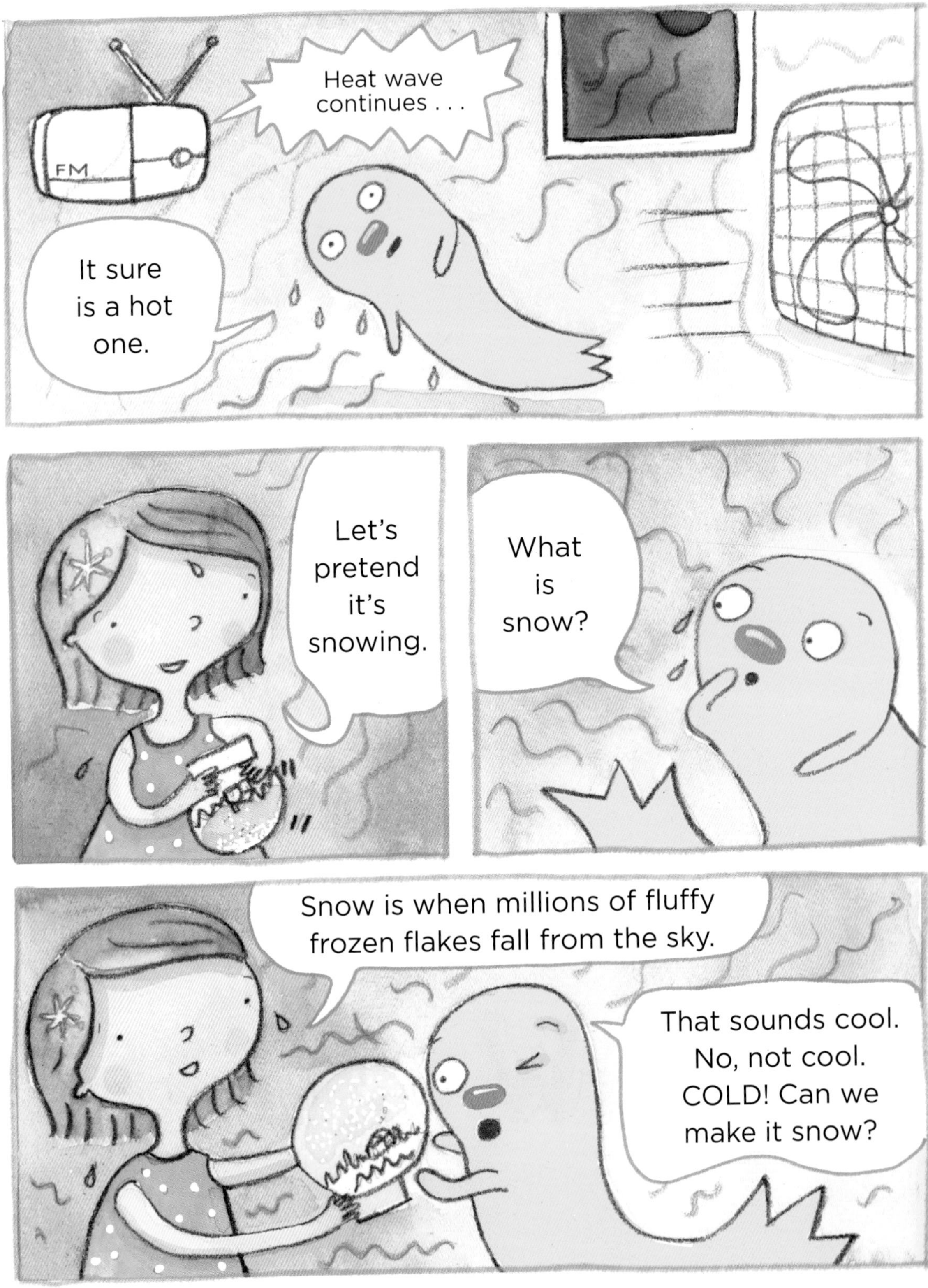
Heat wave continues . . .
FM
It sure is a hot one.
Let's pretend it's snowing.
What is snow?
Snow is when millions of fluffy frozen flakes fall from the sky.
That sounds cool. No, not cool. COLD! Can we make it snow?

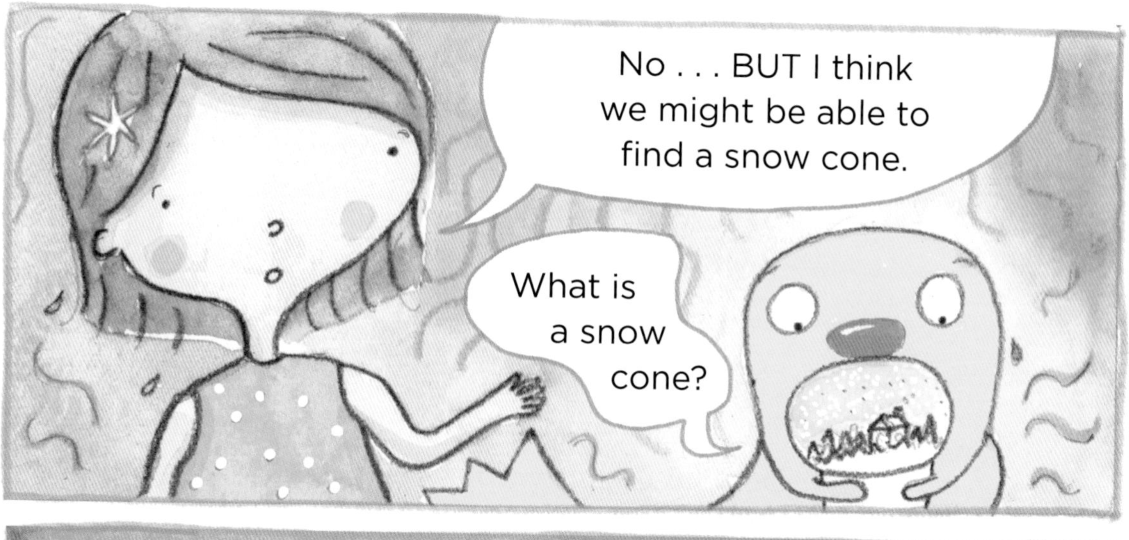
No . . . BUT I think we might be able to find a snow cone.
What is a snow cone?

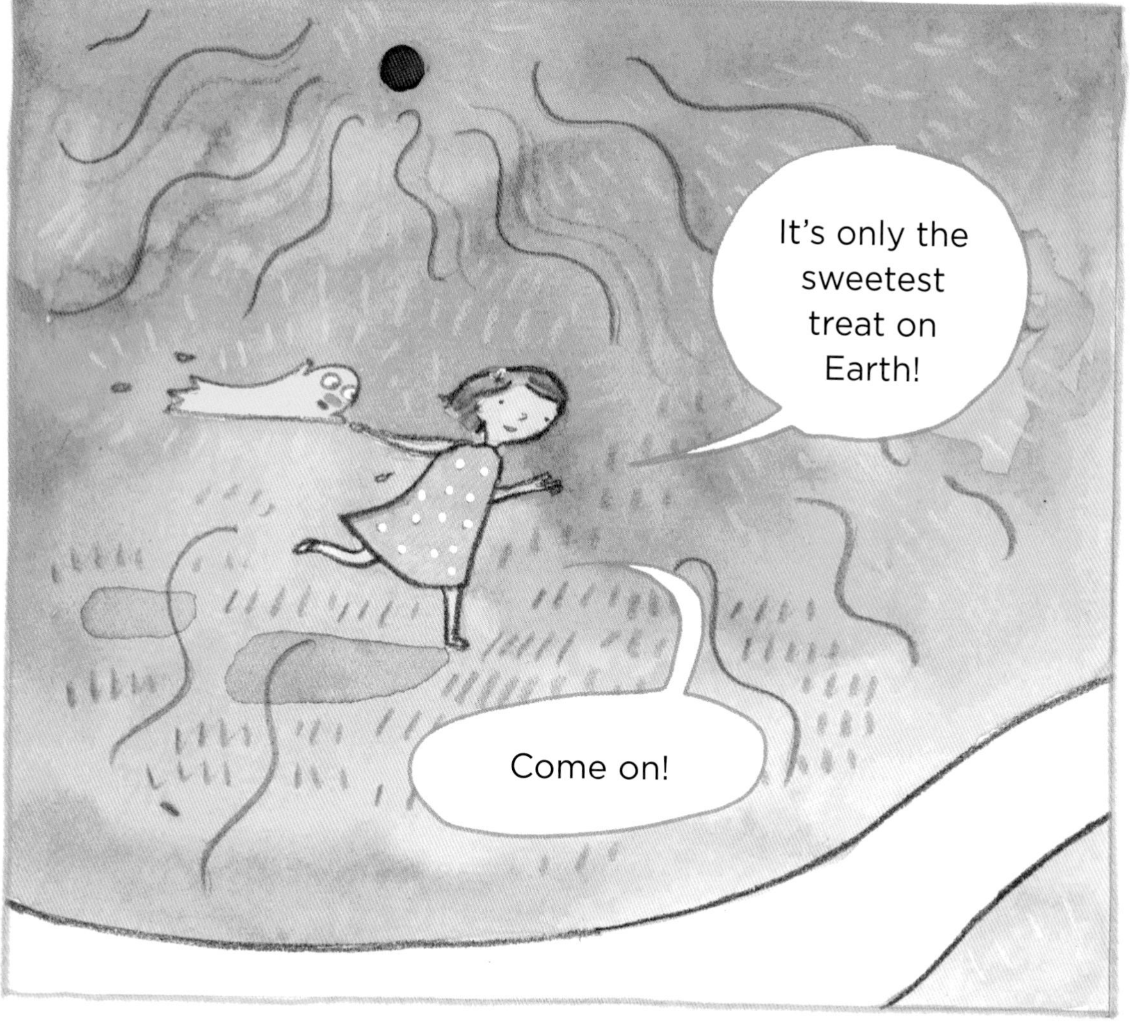
It's only the sweetest treat on Earth!
Come on!

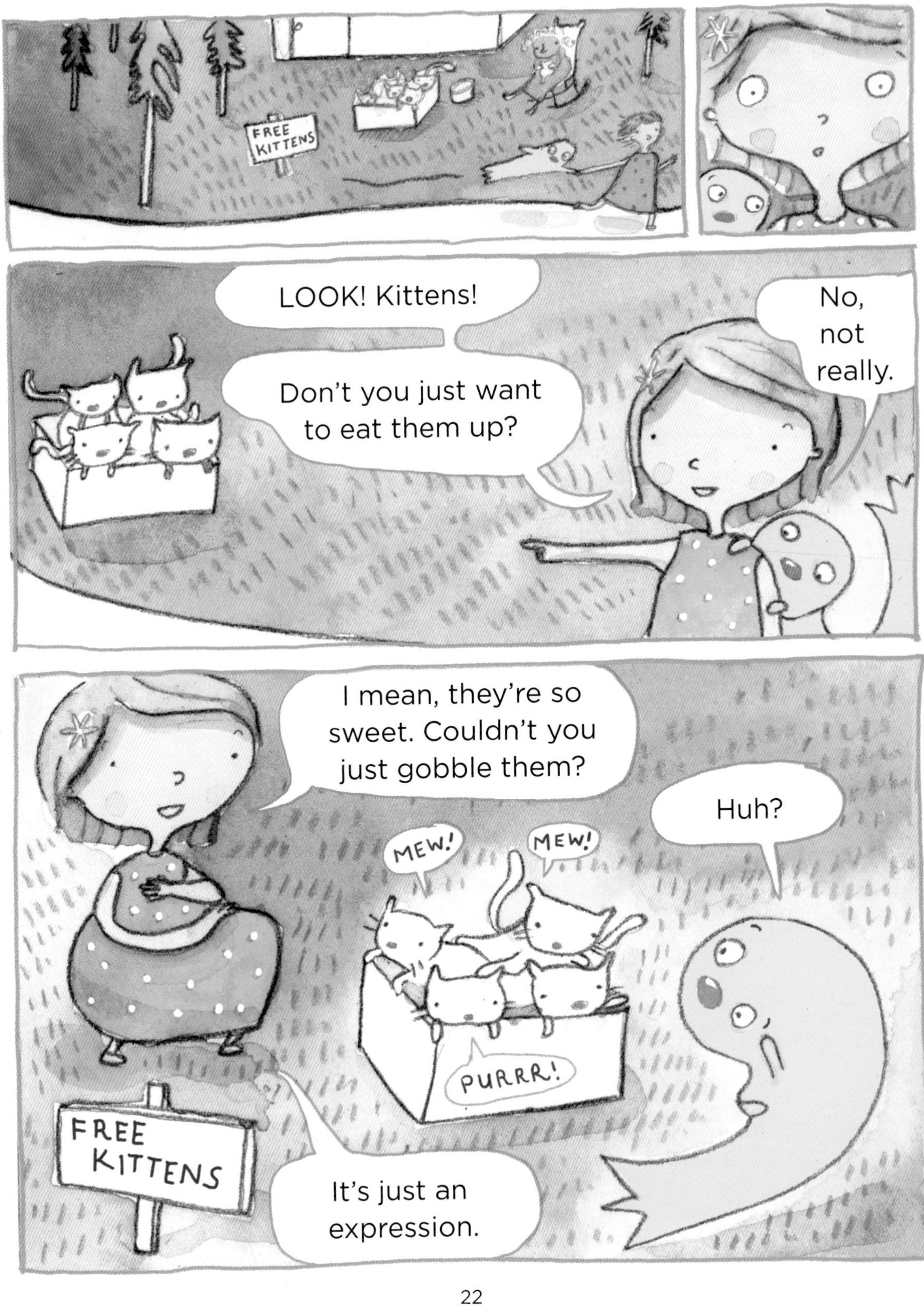
FREE KITTENS
LOOK! Kittens!
Don't you just want to eat them up?
No, not really.
I mean, they're so sweet. Couldn't you just gobble them?
Huh?
MEW!
MEW!
PURRR!
FREE KITTENS
It's just an expression.

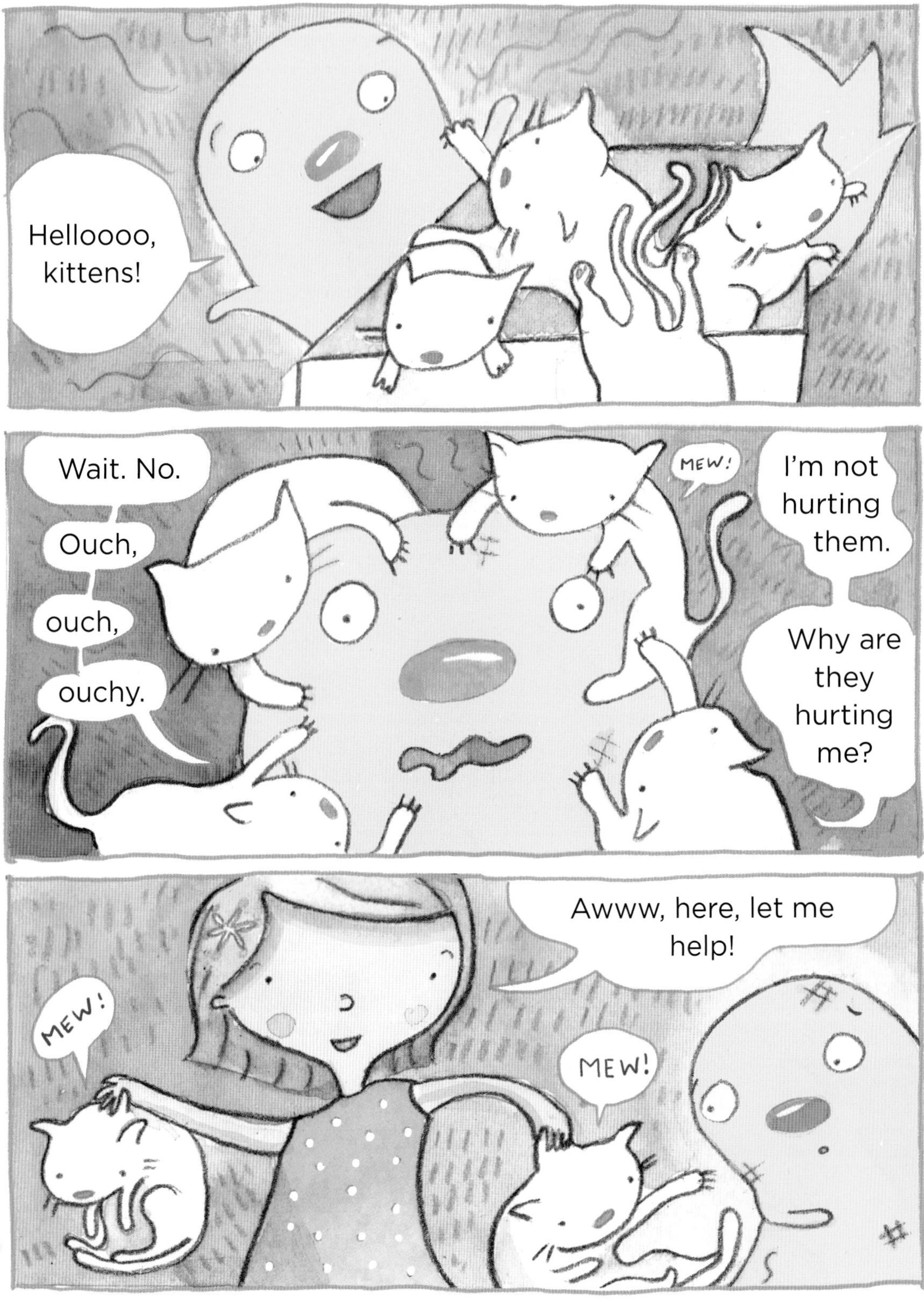
Helloooo, kittens!
Wait. No.
Ouch,
ouch,
ouchy.
MEW!
I'm not hurting them.
Why are they hurting me?
Awww, here, let me help!
MEW!
MEW!

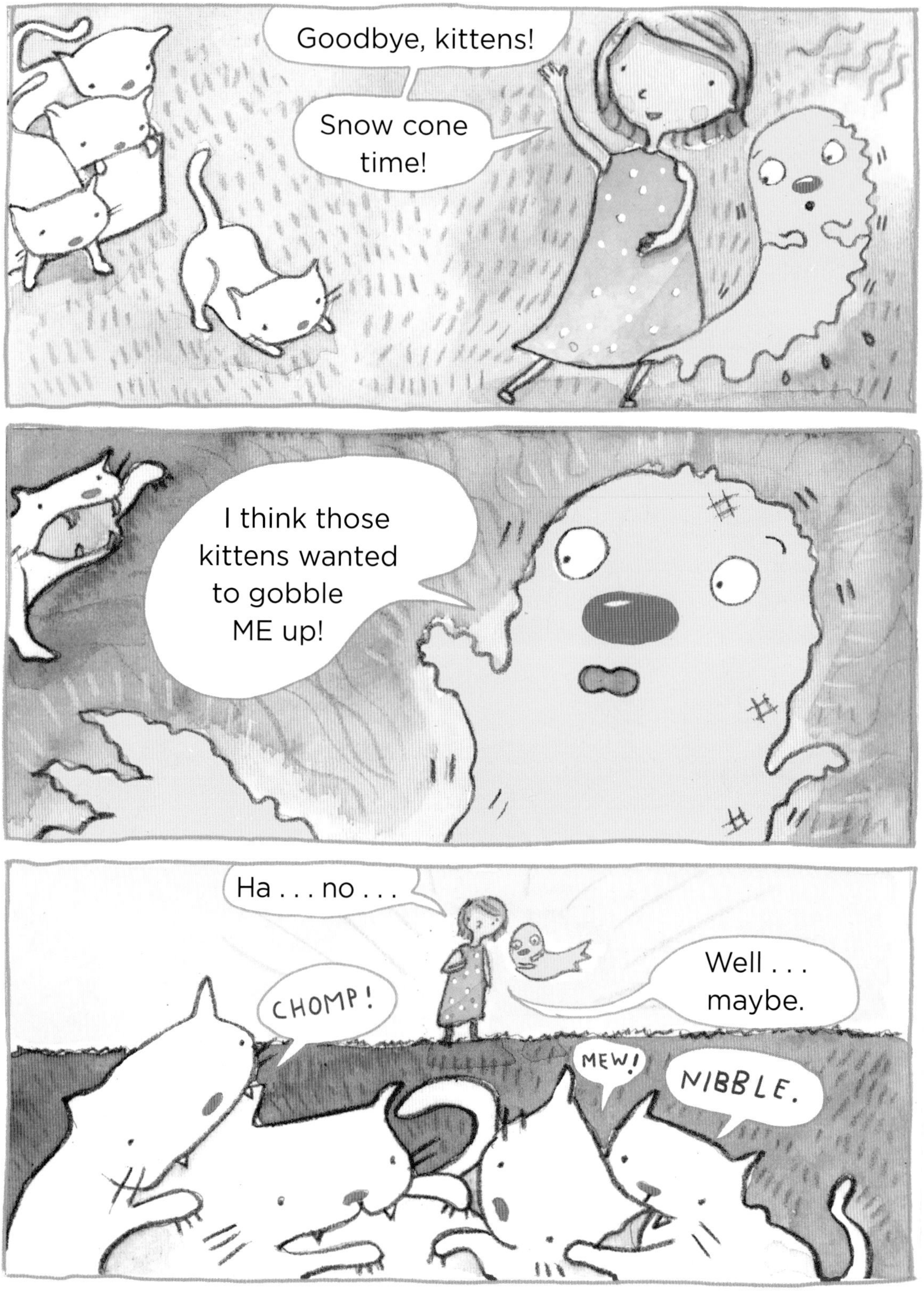
Goodbye, kittens!
Snow cone time!
I think those kittens wanted to gobble ME up!
Ha . . . no . . .
Well . . . maybe.
CHOMP!
MEW!
NIBBLE.

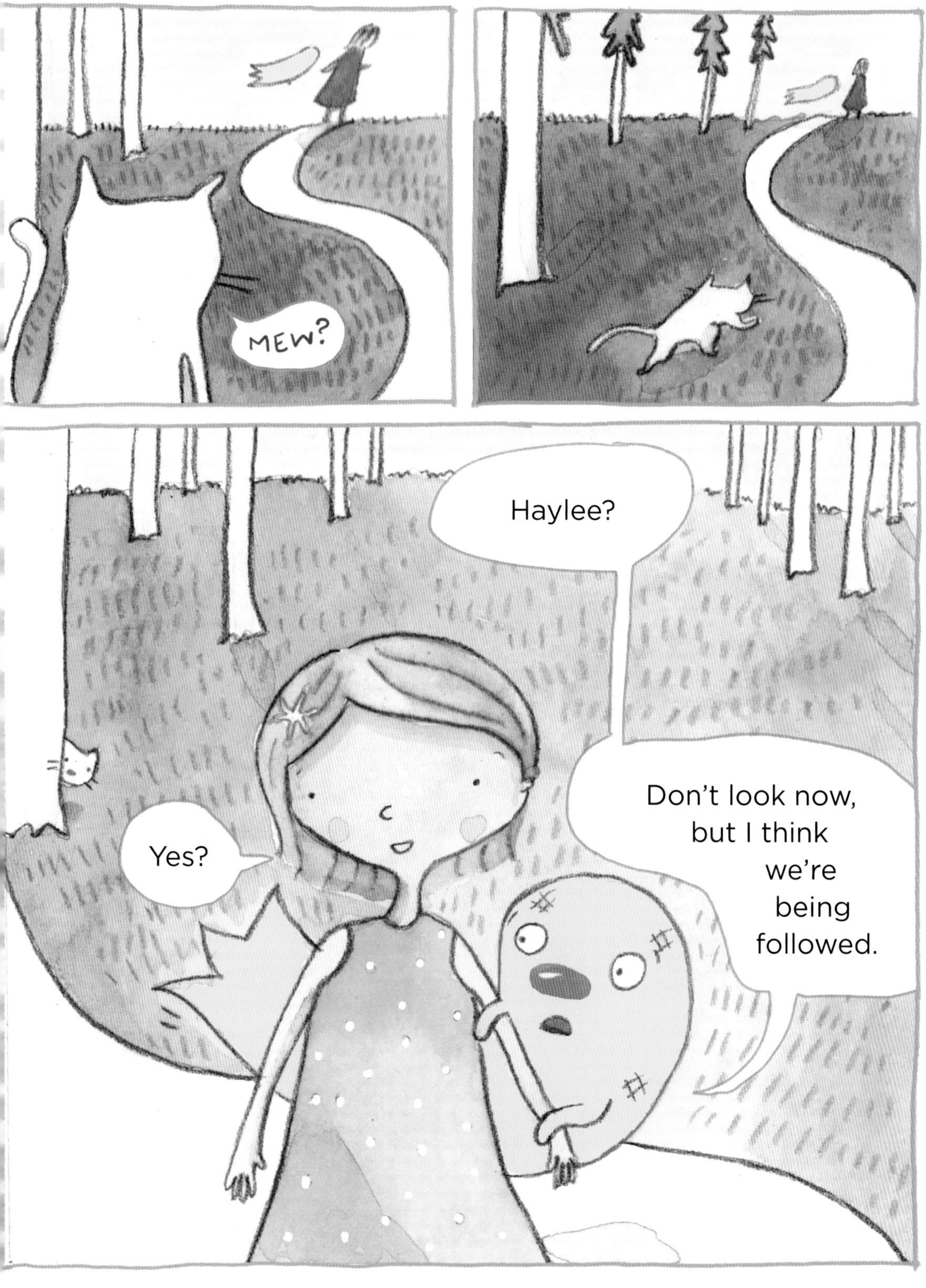

MEW?
Haylee?
Yes?
Don't look now, but I think we're being followed.

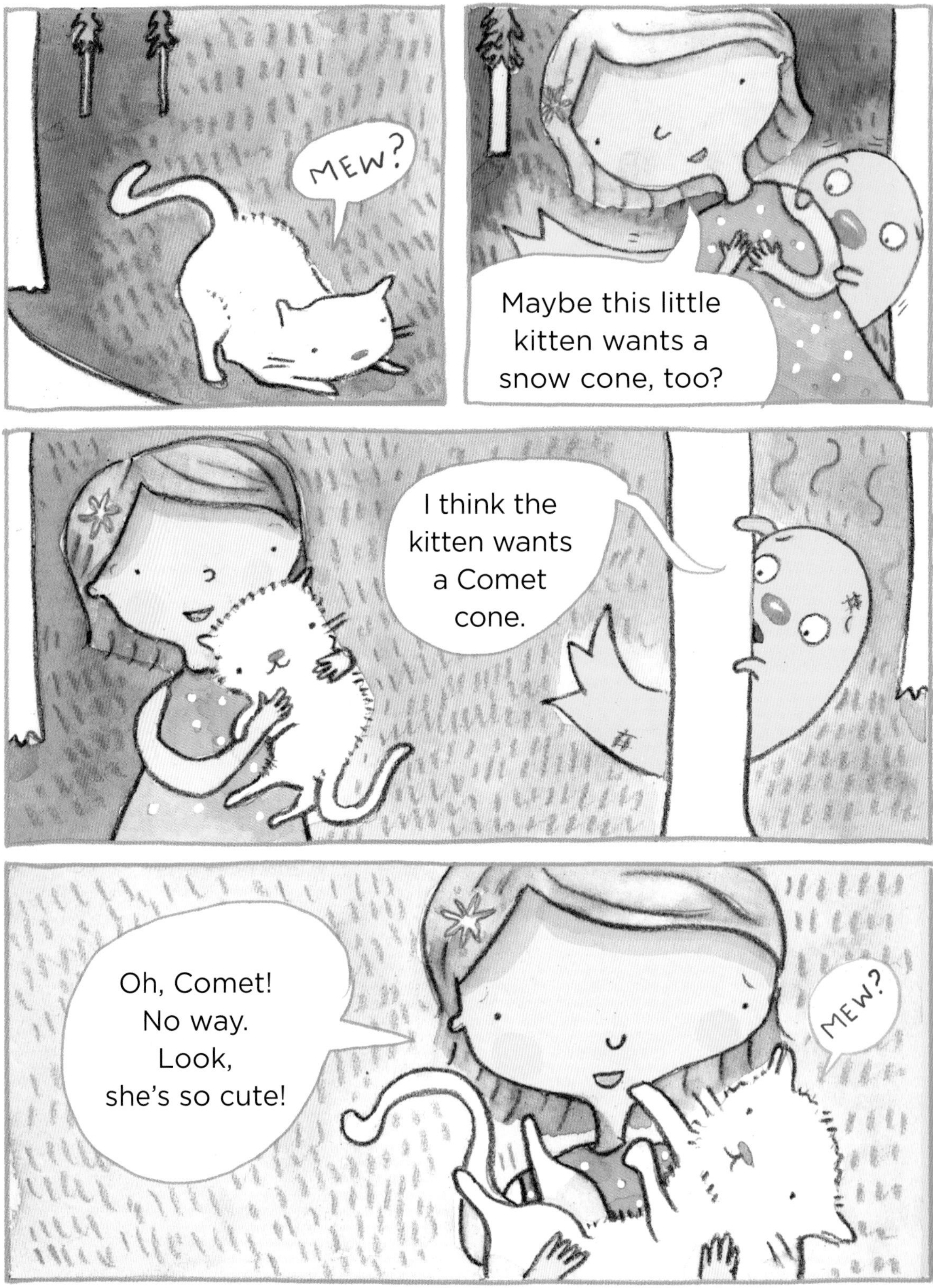
MEW?
Maybe this little kitten wants a snow cone, too?
I think the kitten wants a Comet cone.
Oh, Comet! No way. Look, she's so cute!
MEW?

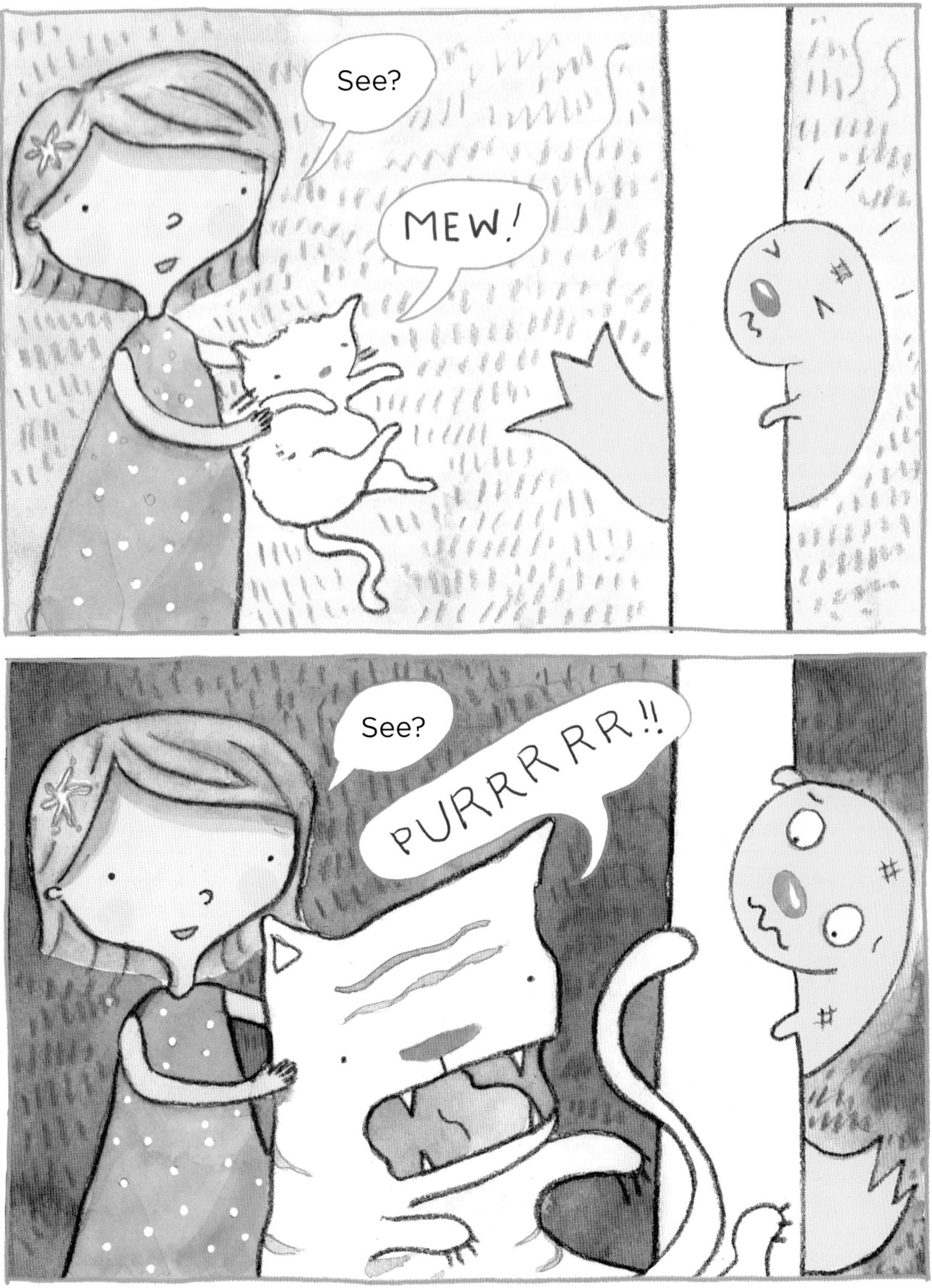
See?
MEW!
See?
PURRRRR!!

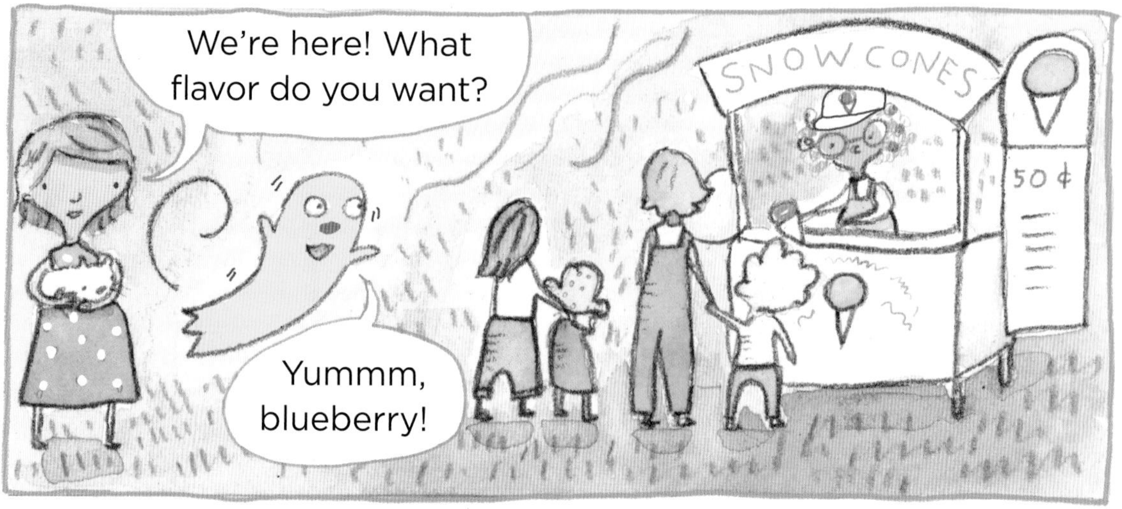
We're here! What flavor do you want?
SNOW CONES
50¢
Yummm, blueberry!

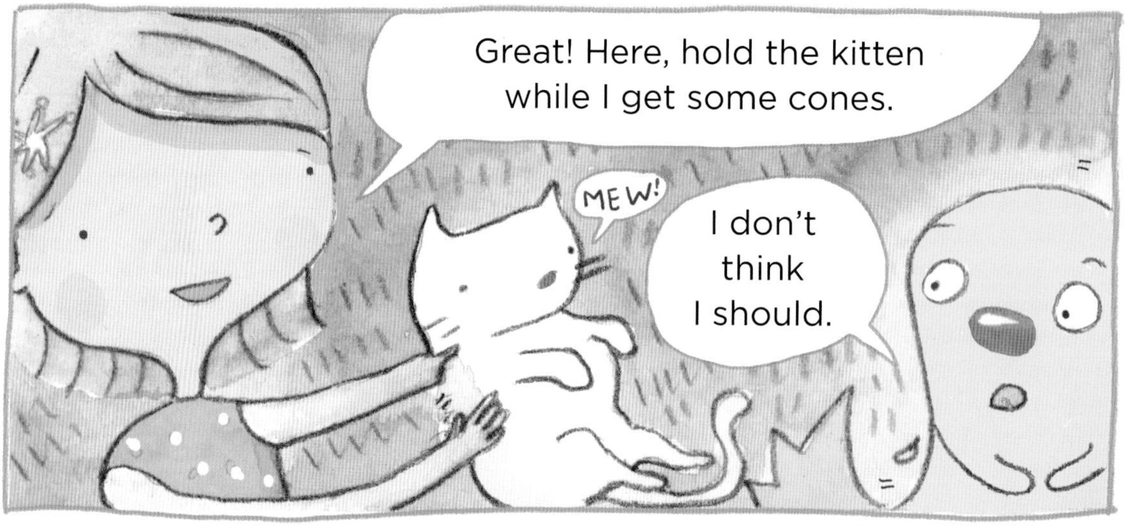
Great! Here, hold the kitten while I get some cones.
MEW!
I don't think I should.

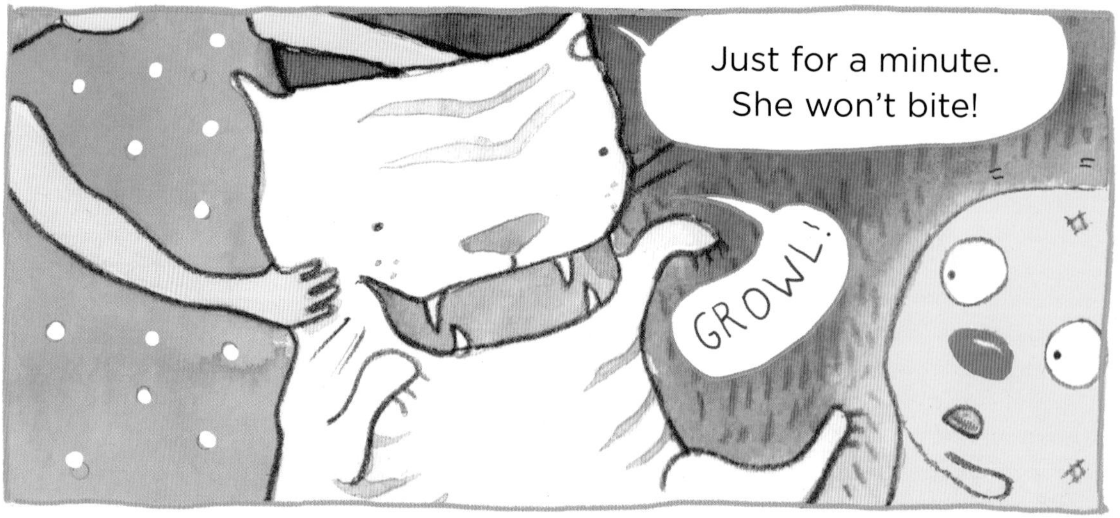
Just for a minute. She won't bite!
GROWL!

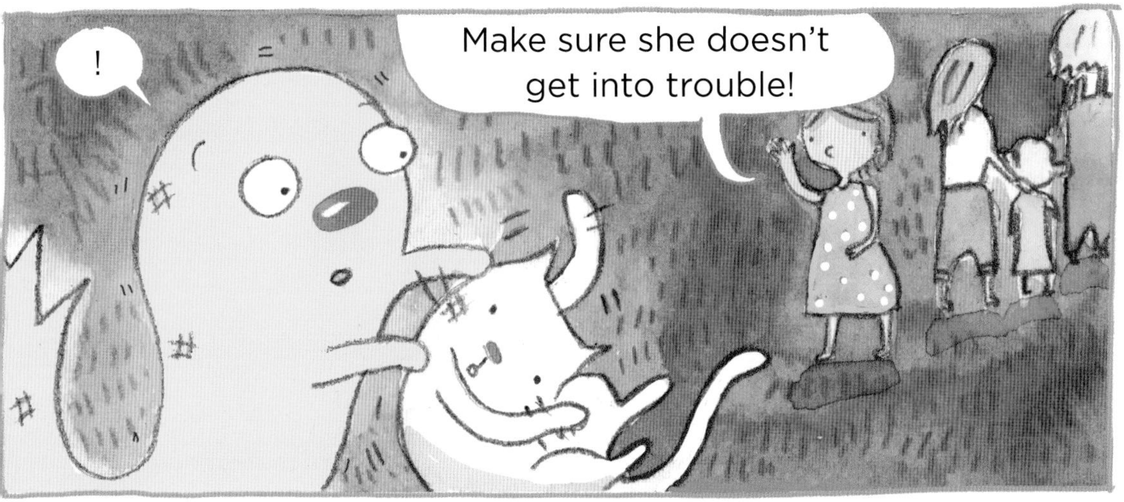
!
Make sure she doesn't get into trouble!

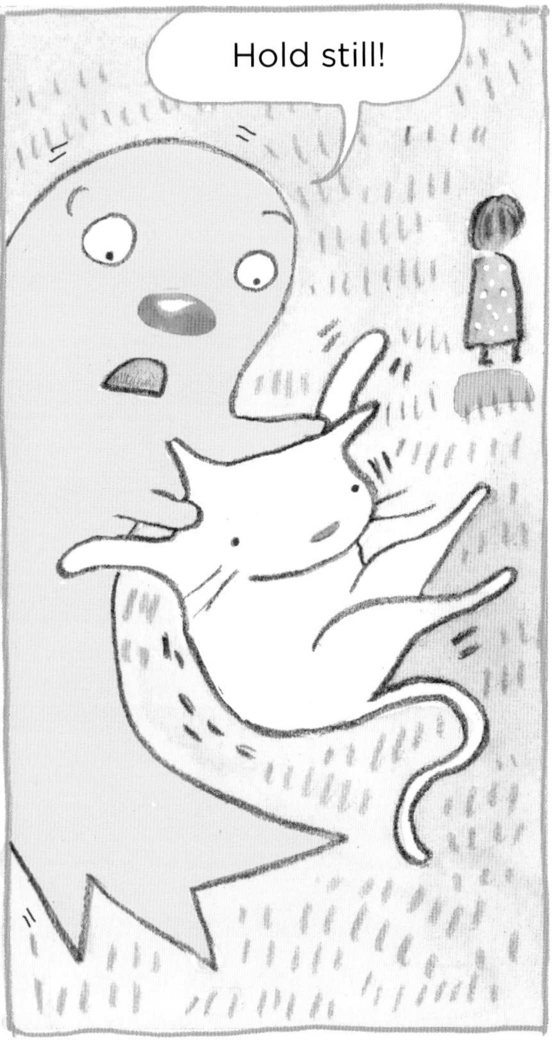
Hold still!

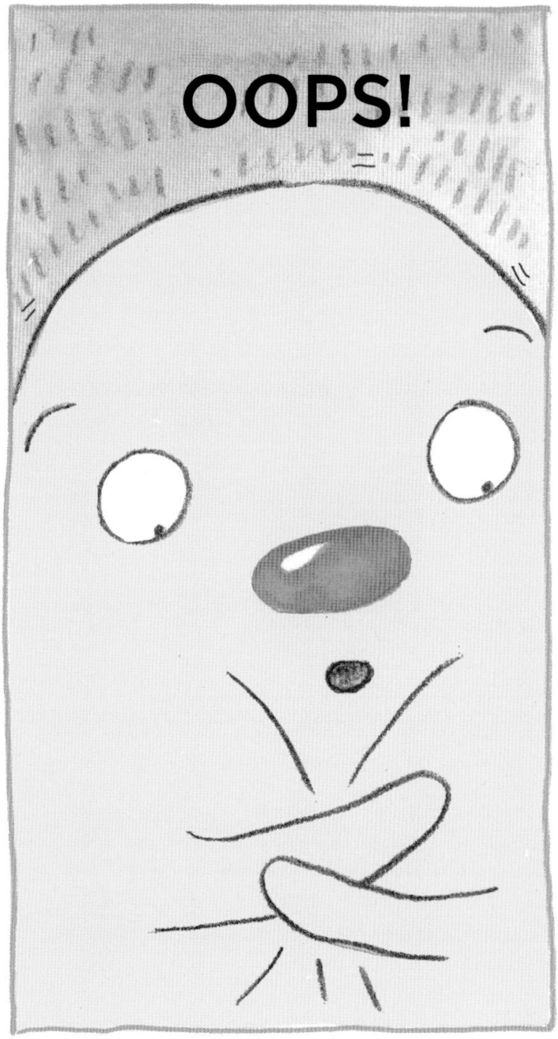
OOPS!

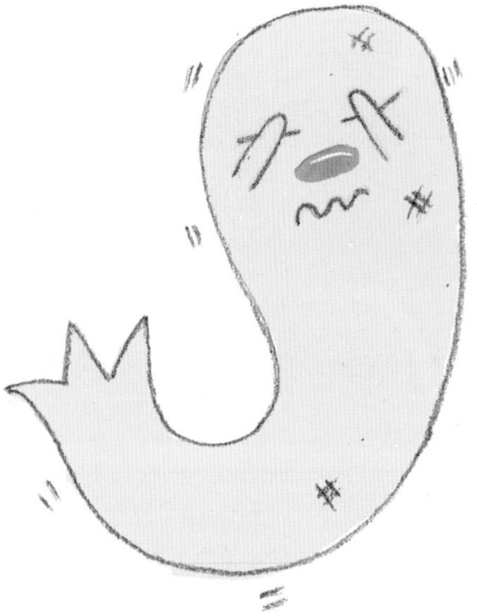

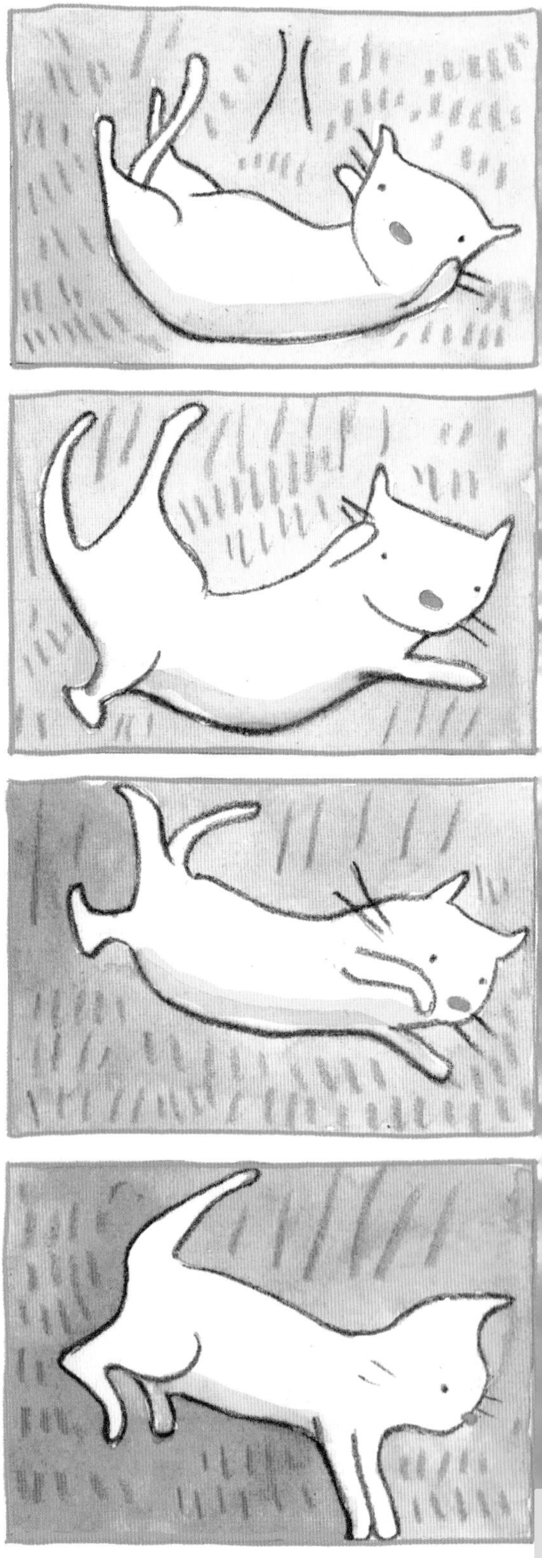

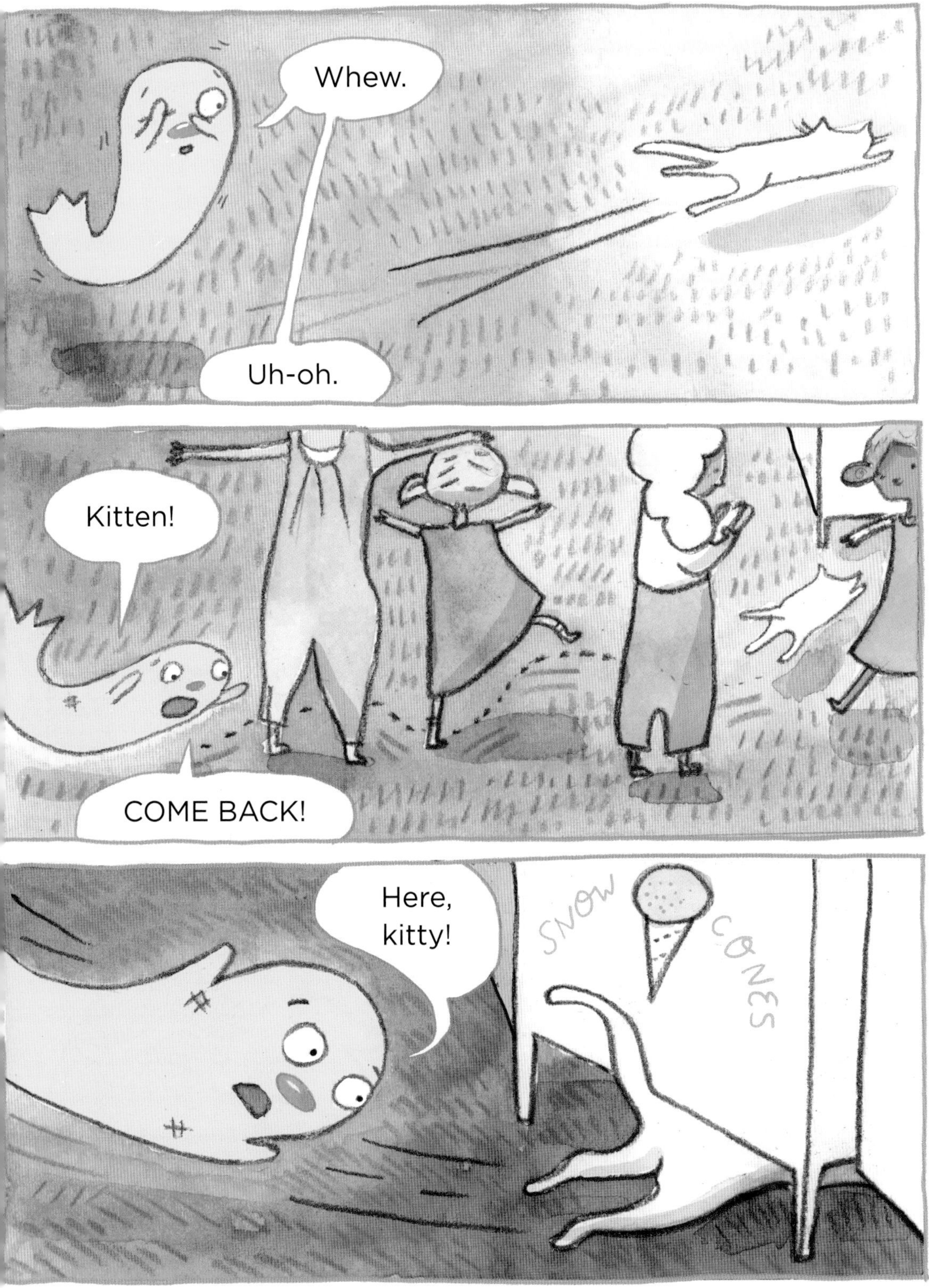
Whew.
Uh-oh.
Kitten!
COME BACK!
Here, kitty!
SNOW CONES

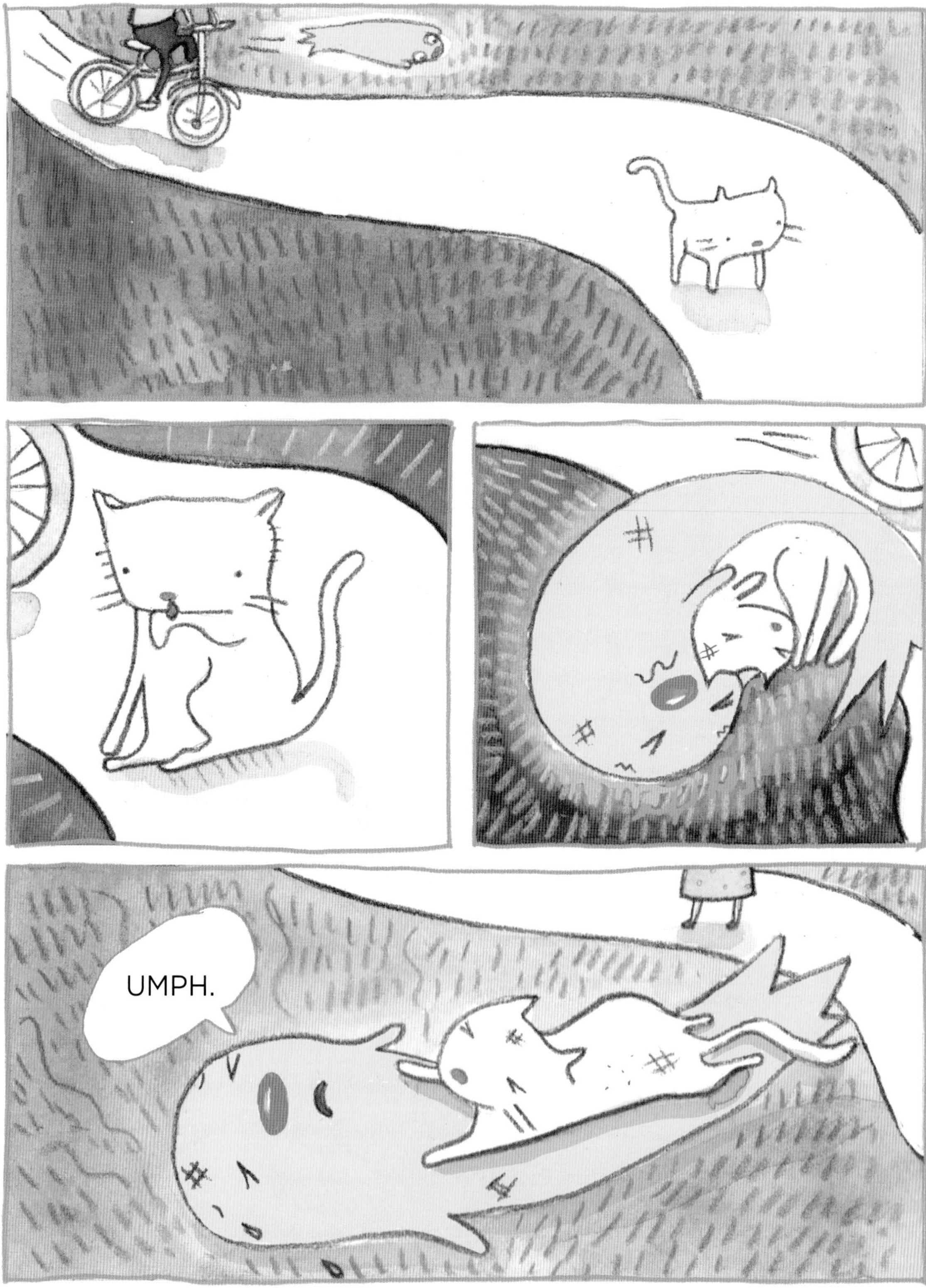
UMPH.

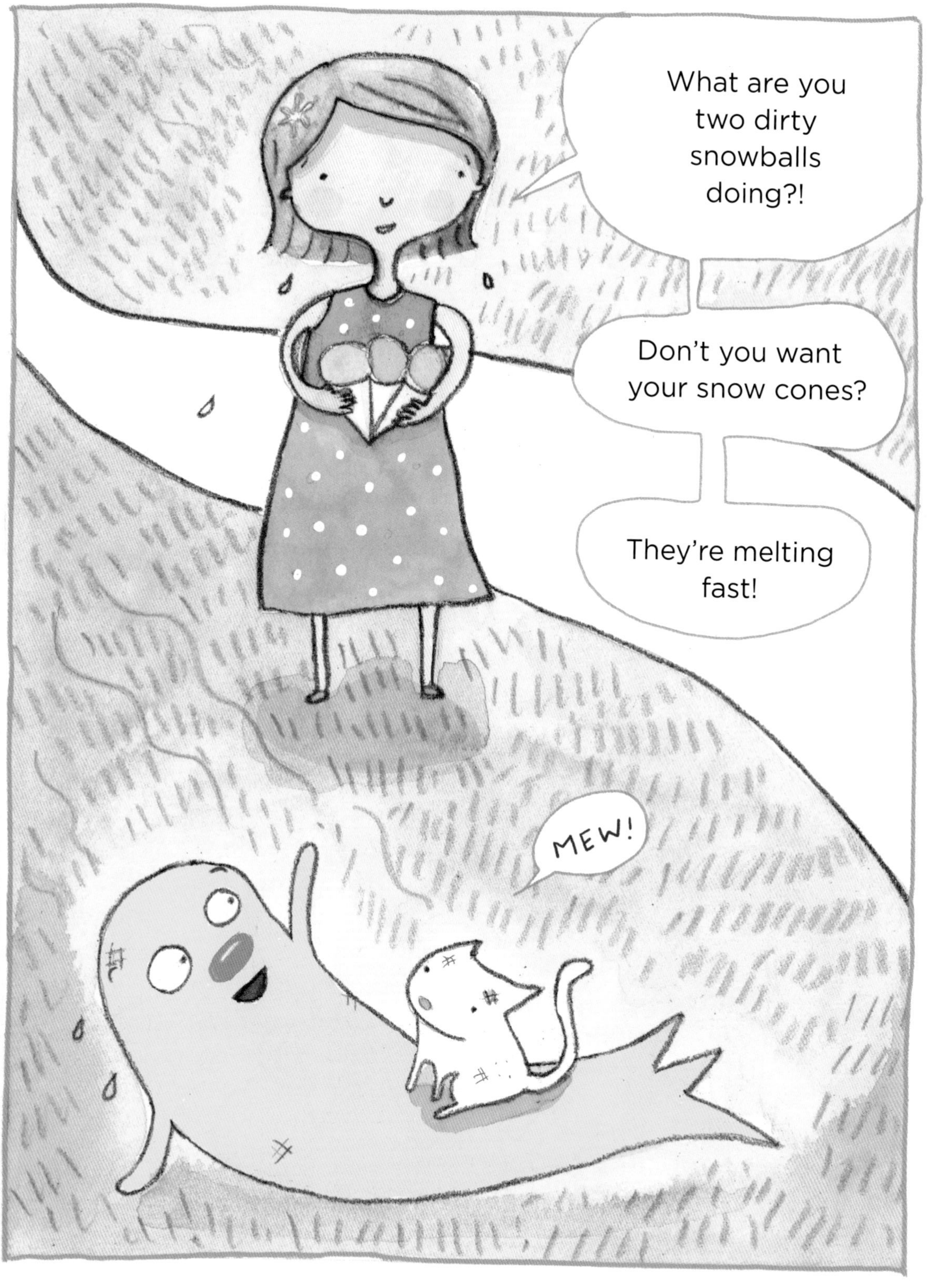
What are you two dirty snowballs doing?!
Don't you want your snow cones?
They're melting fast!
MEW!

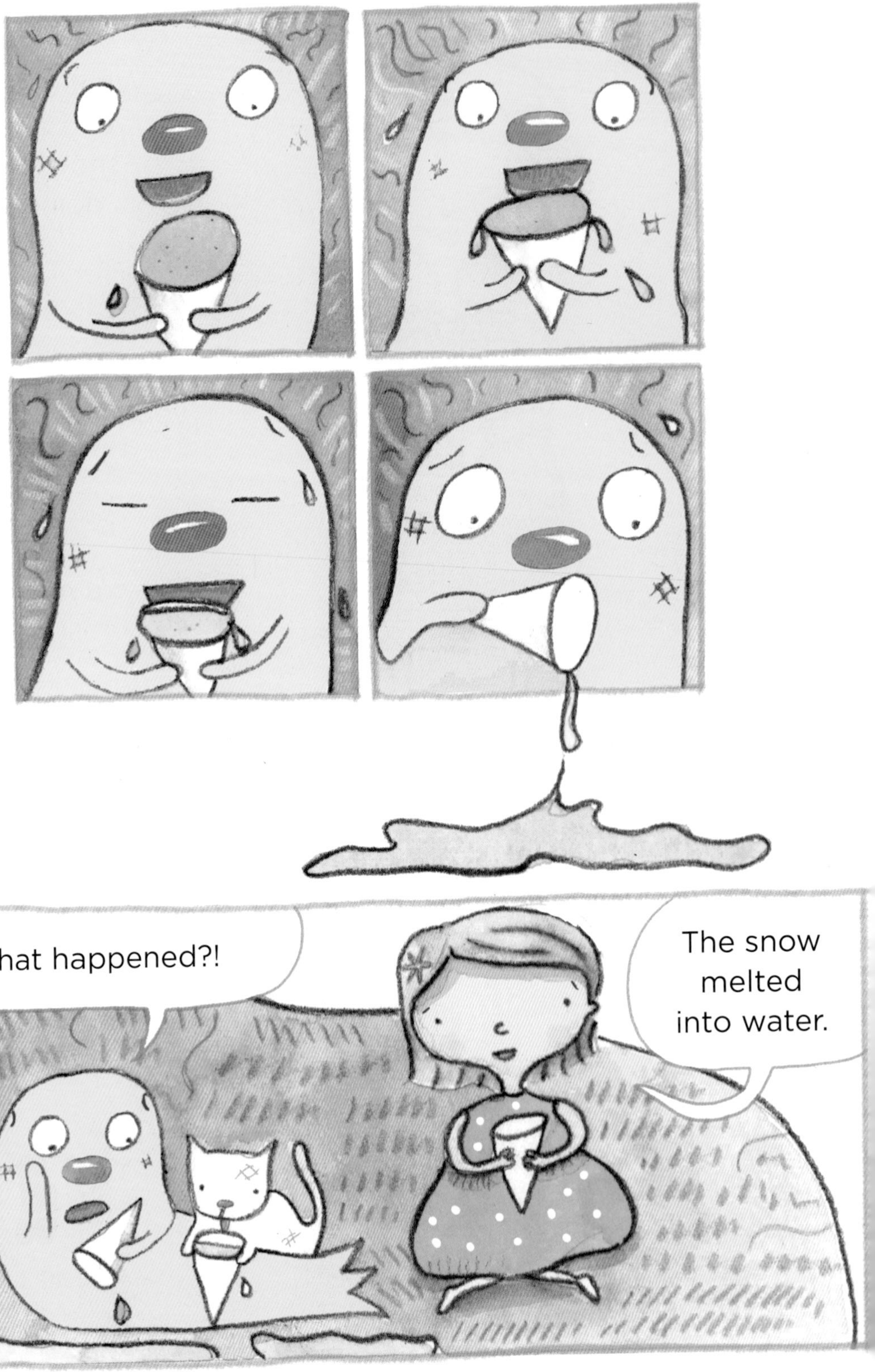
What happened?!
The snow melted into water.

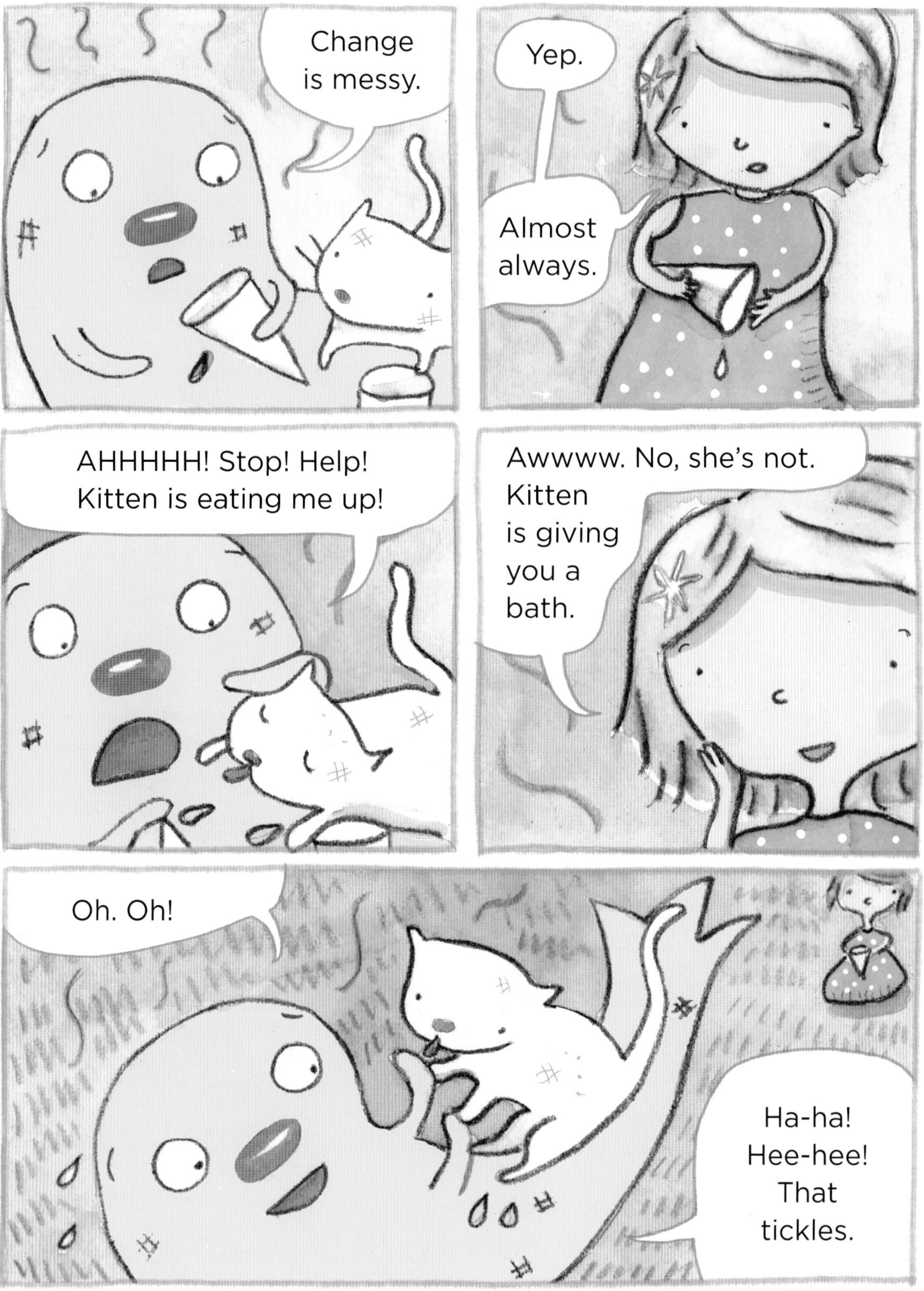
Change is messy.
Yep.
Almost always.
AHHHHH! Stop! Help! Kitten is eating me up!
Awwww. No, she's not. Kitten is giving you a bath.
Oh. Oh!
Ha-ha! Hee-hee! That tickles.

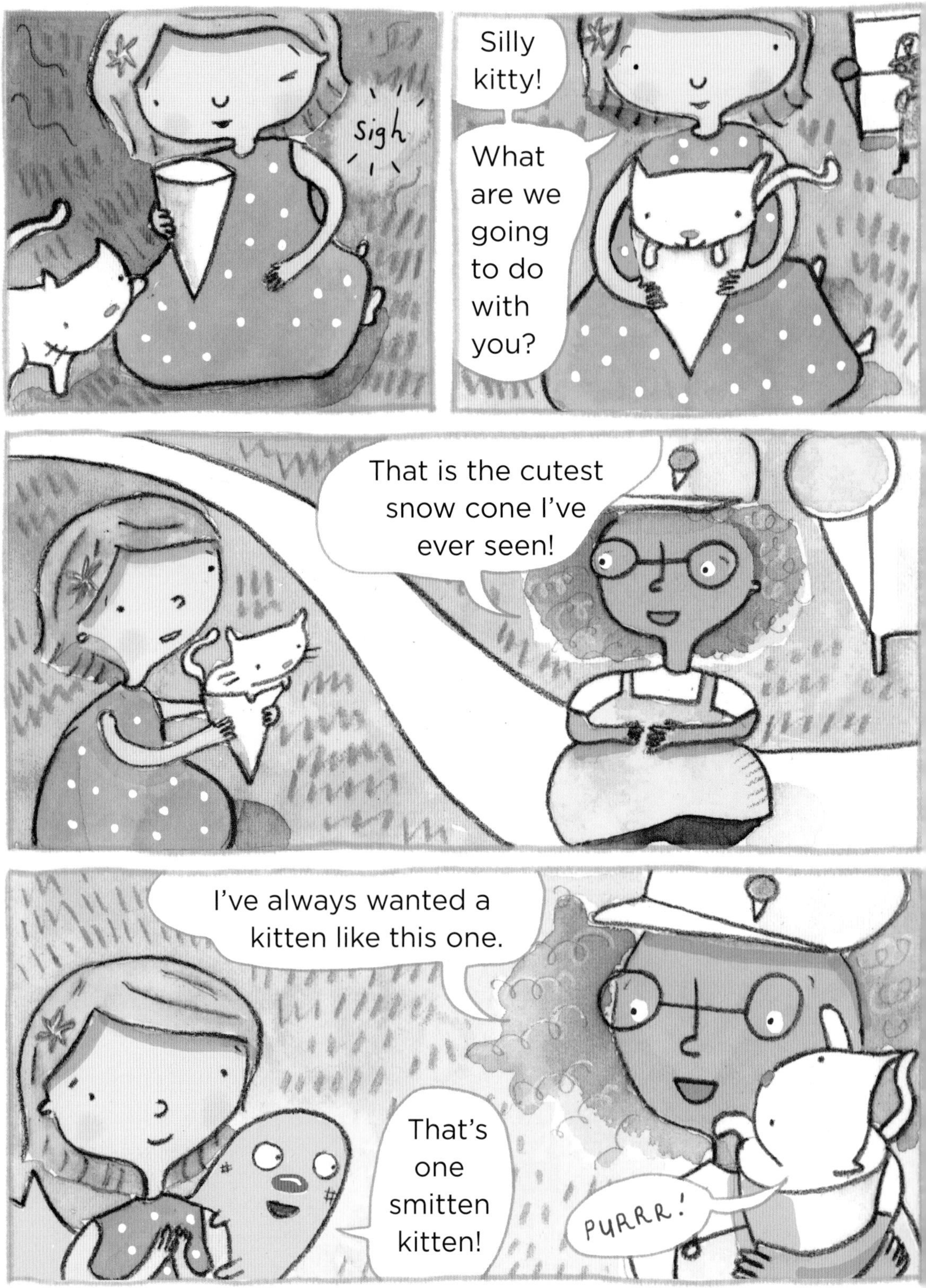
Sigh
Silly kitty!
What are we going to do with you?
That is the cutest snow cone I've ever seen!
I've always wanted a kitten like this one.
That's one smitten kitten!
PURRR!

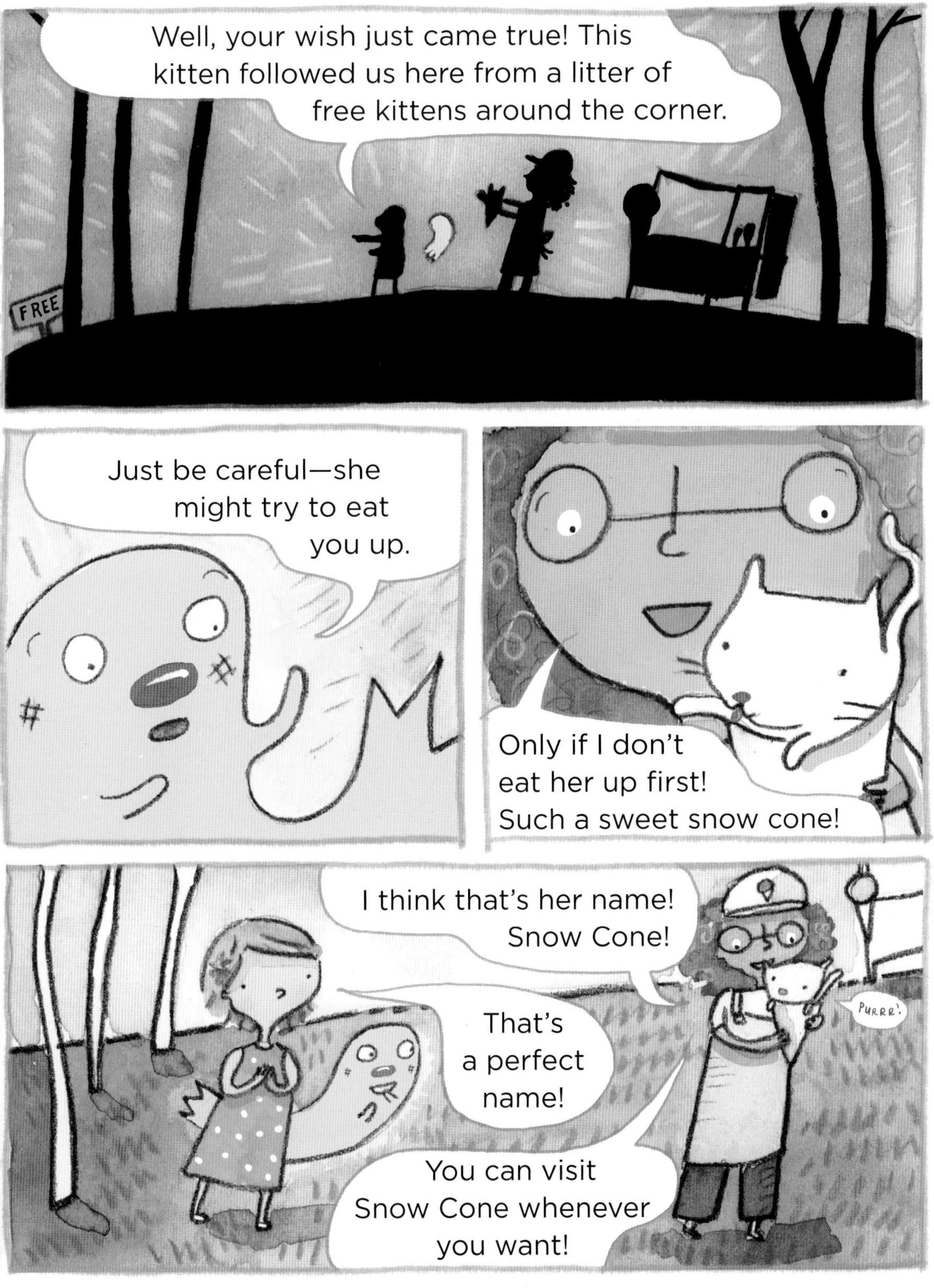
FREE
Well, your wish just came true! This kitten followed us here from a litter of free kittens around the corner.
Just be careful—she might try to eat you up.
Only if I don't eat her up first! Such a sweet snow cone!
I think that's her name! Snow Cone!
That's a perfect name!
PURRR!
You can visit Snow Cone whenever you want!

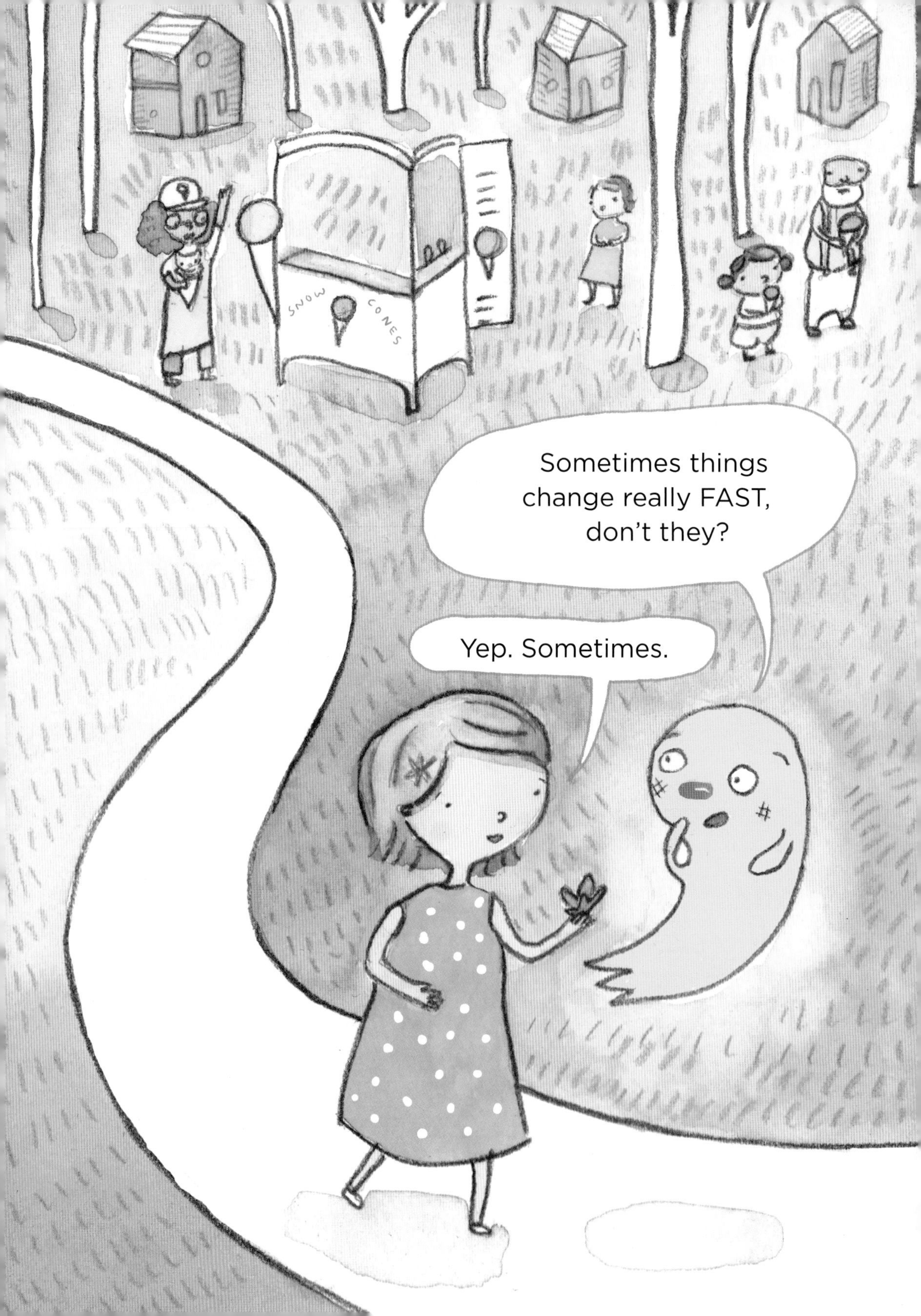
SNOW CONES
Sometimes things change really FAST, don't they?
Yep. Sometimes.

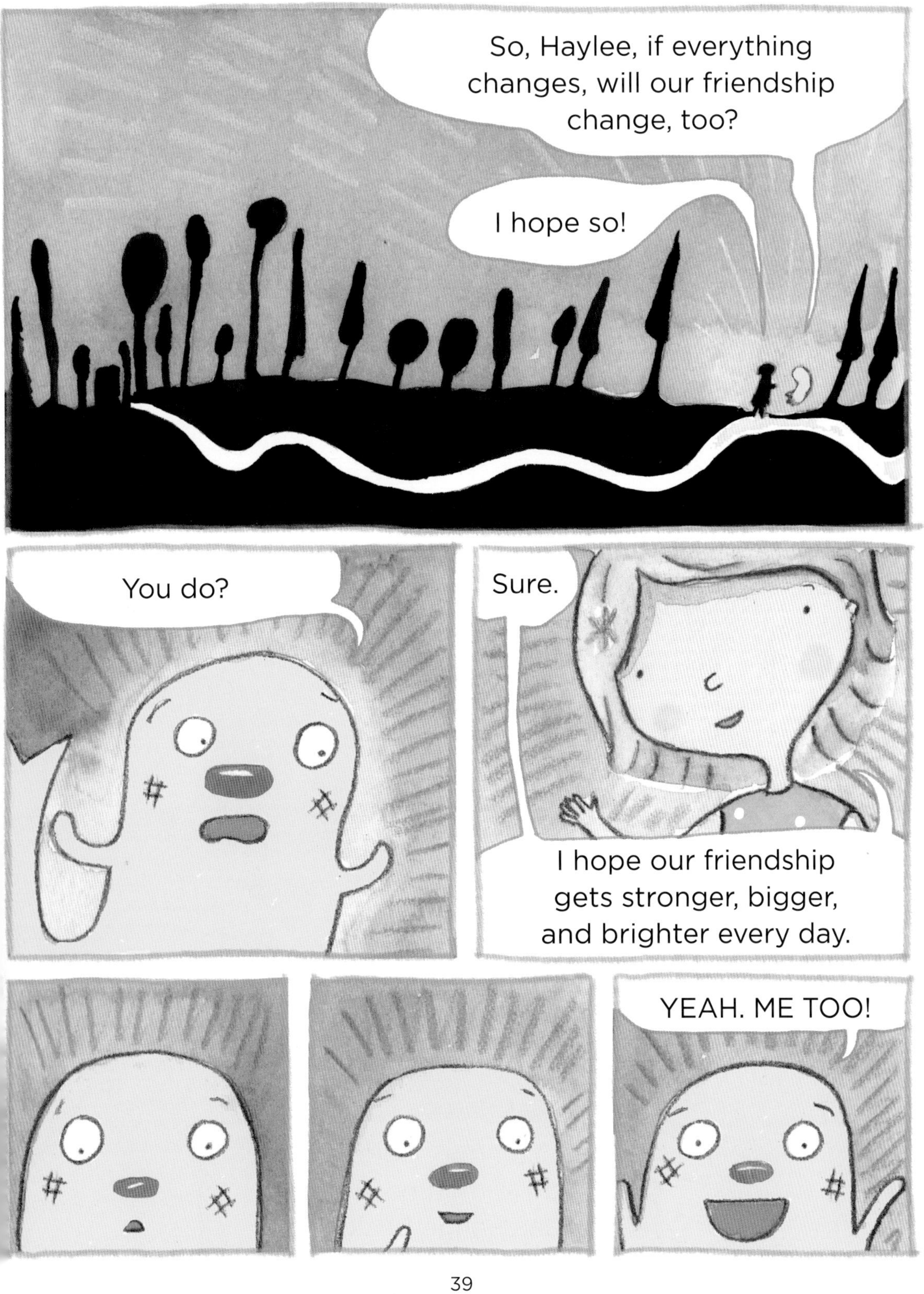
So, Haylee, if everything changes, will our friendship change, too?
I hope so!
You do?
Sure.
I hope our friendship gets stronger, bigger, and brighter every day.
YEAH. ME TOO!

Can things ever change back?

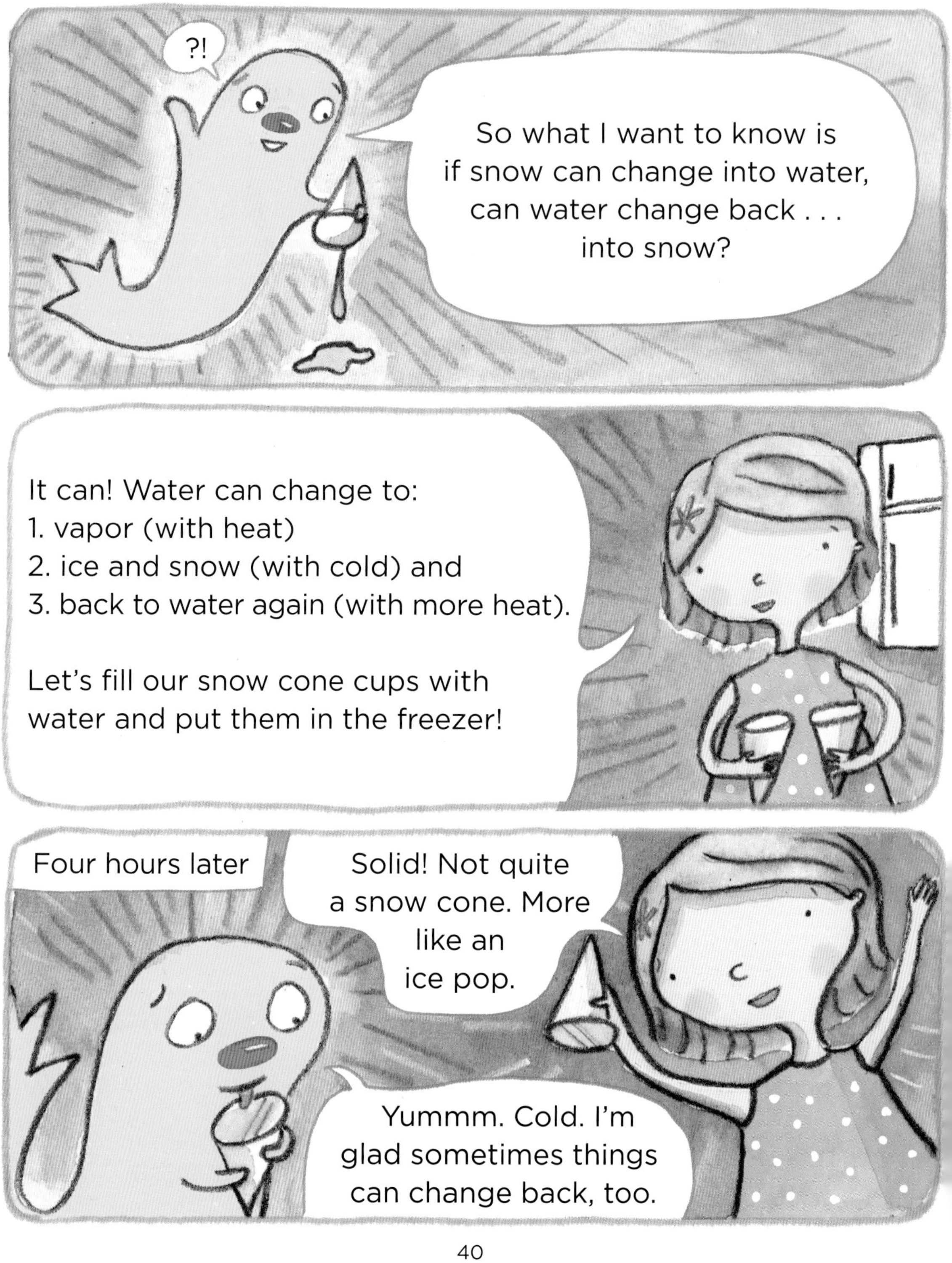
?!
So what I want to know is if snow can change into water, can water change back . . . into snow?
It can! Water can change to:
1. vapor (with heat)
2. ice and snow (with cold) and
3. back to water again (with more heat).
Let's fill our snow cone cups with water and put them in the freezer!
Four hours later
Solid! Not quite a snow cone. More like an ice pop.
Yummm. Cold. I'm glad sometimes things can change back, too.

GROWING UP

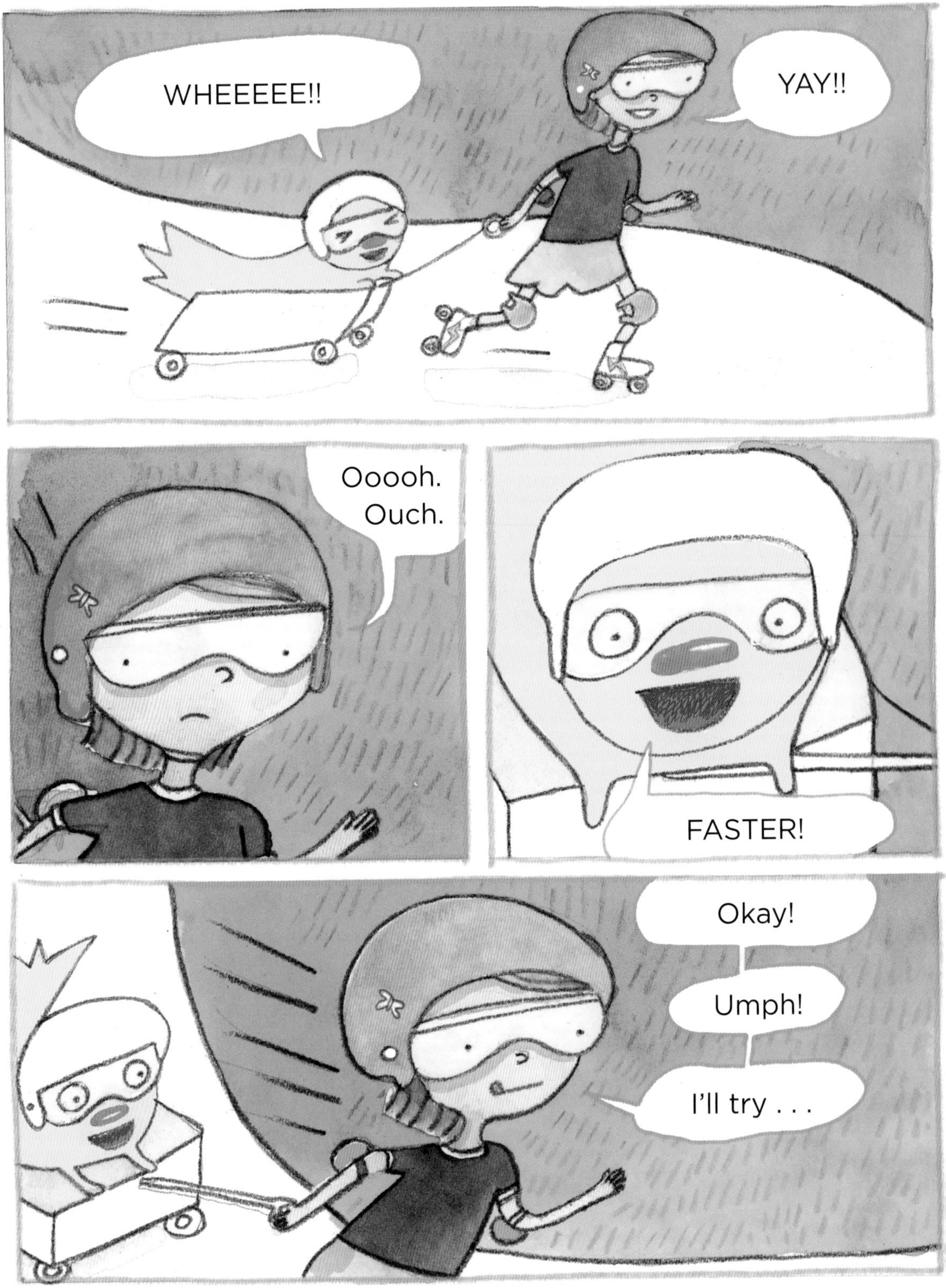
WHEEEEE!!
YAY!!
Ooooh.
Ouch.
FASTER!
Okay!
Umph!
I'll try . . .

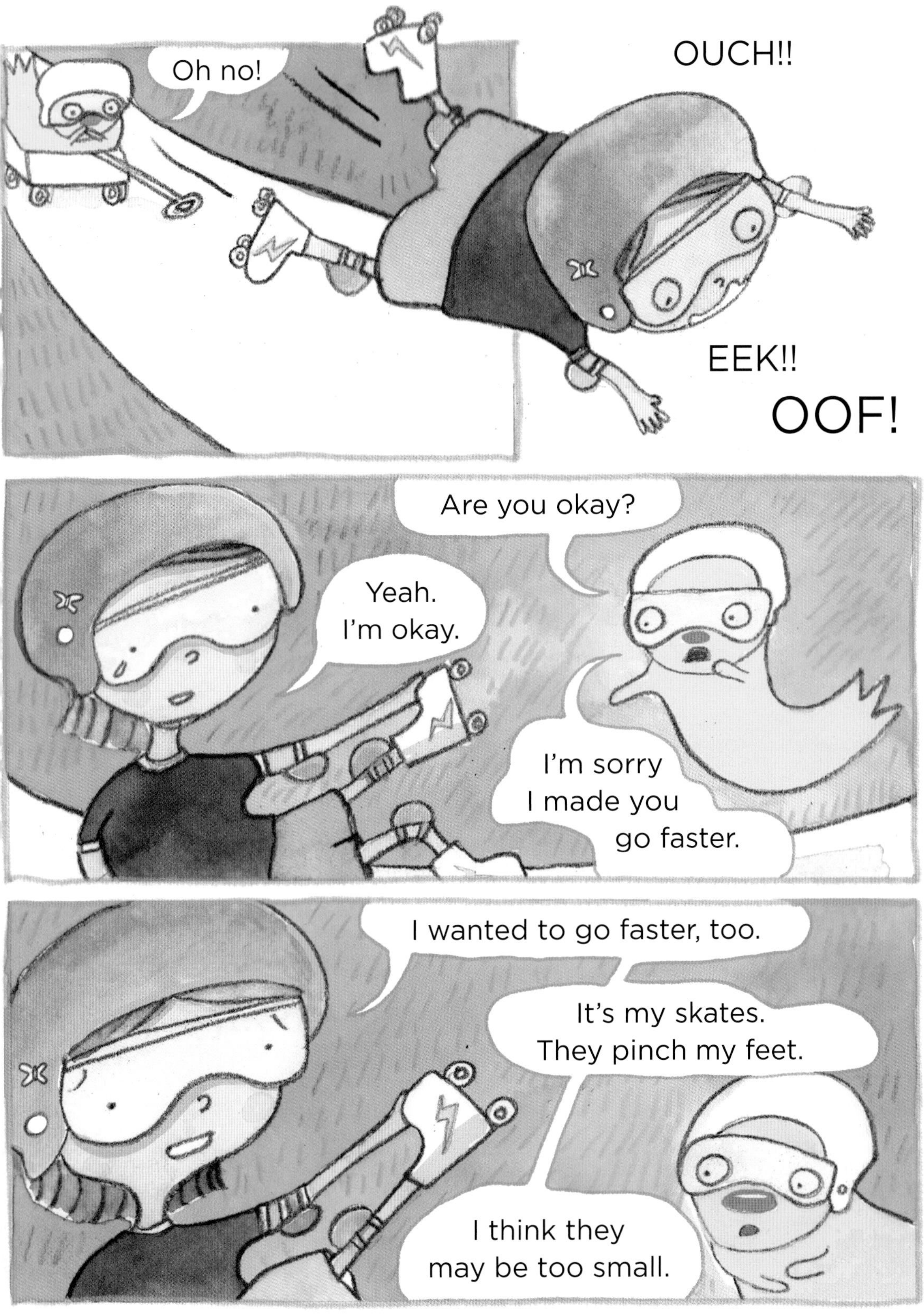
Oh no!
OUCH!!
EEK!!
OOF!
Are you okay?
Yeah. I'm okay.
I'm sorry I made you go faster.
I wanted to go faster, too.
It's my skates. They pinch my feet.
I think they may be too small.

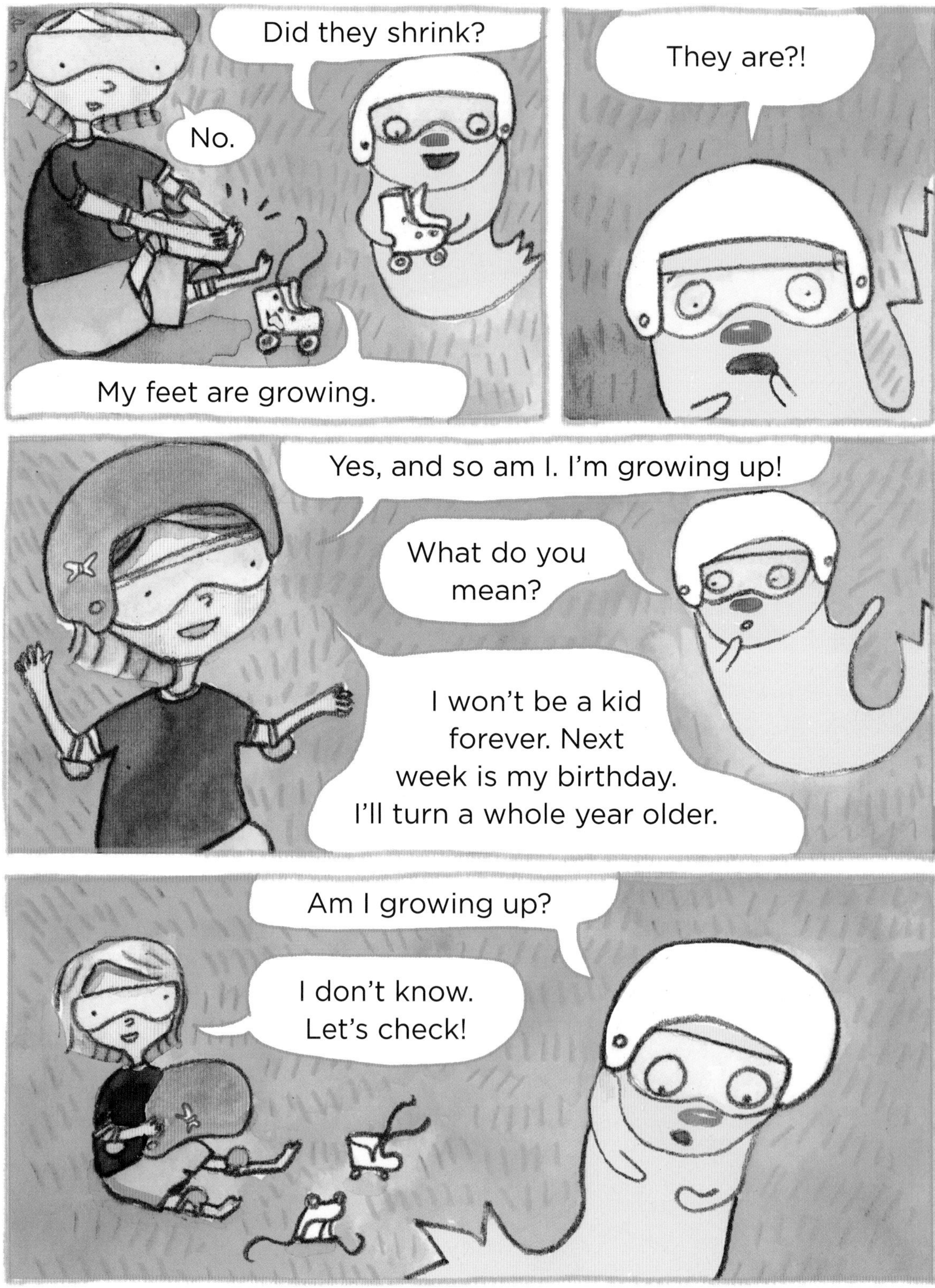
Did they shrink?
No.
My feet are growing.
They are?!
Yes, and so am I. I'm growing up!
What do you mean?
I won't be a kid forever. Next week is my birthday. I'll turn a whole year older.
Am I growing up?
I don't know. Let's check!

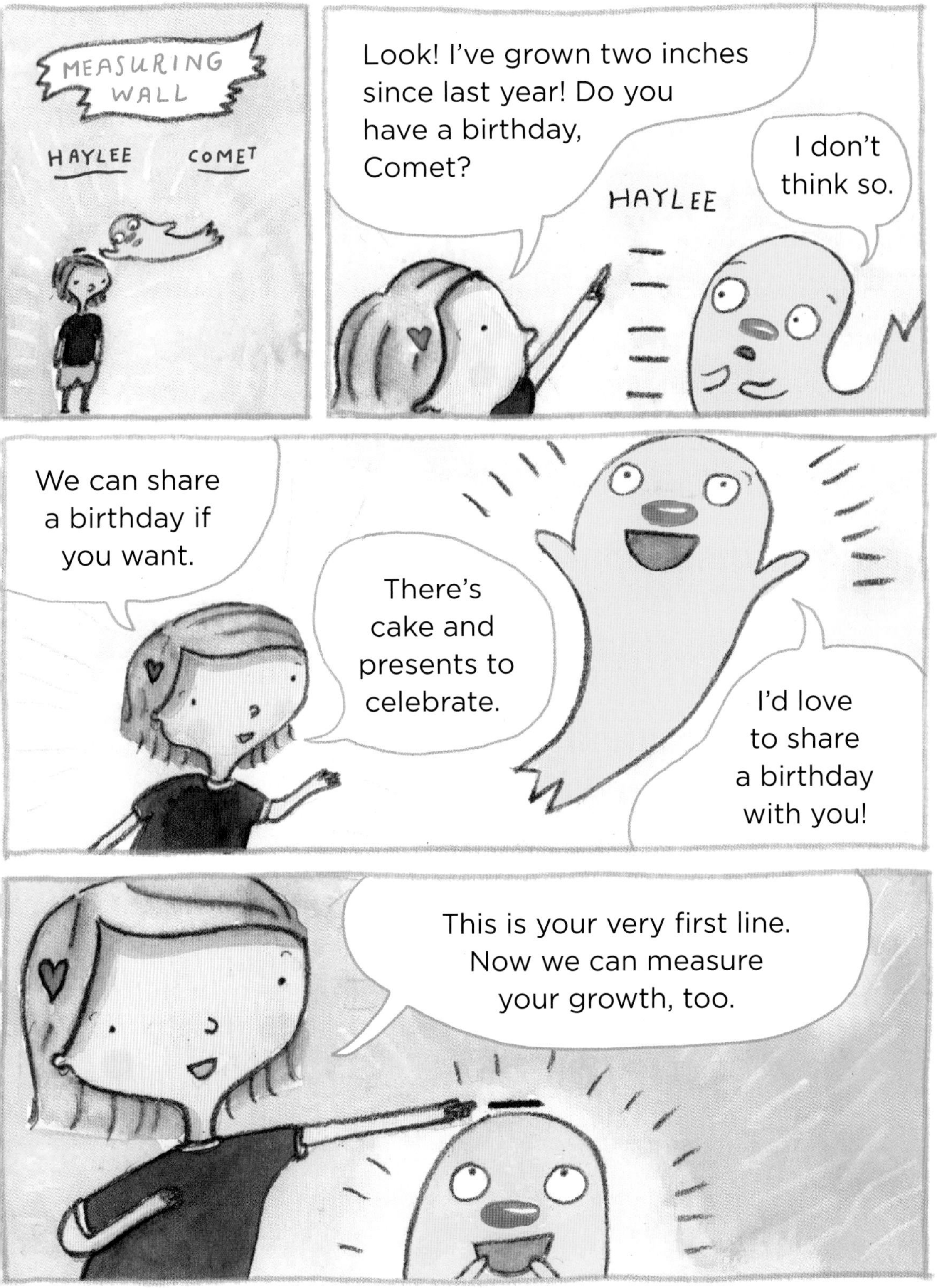
MEASURING WALL
HAYLEE
COMET
Look! I've grown two inches since last year! Do you have a birthday, Comet?
HAYLEE
I don't think so.
We can share a birthday if you want.
There's cake and presents to celebrate.
I'd love to share a birthday with you!
This is your very first line. Now we can measure your growth, too.

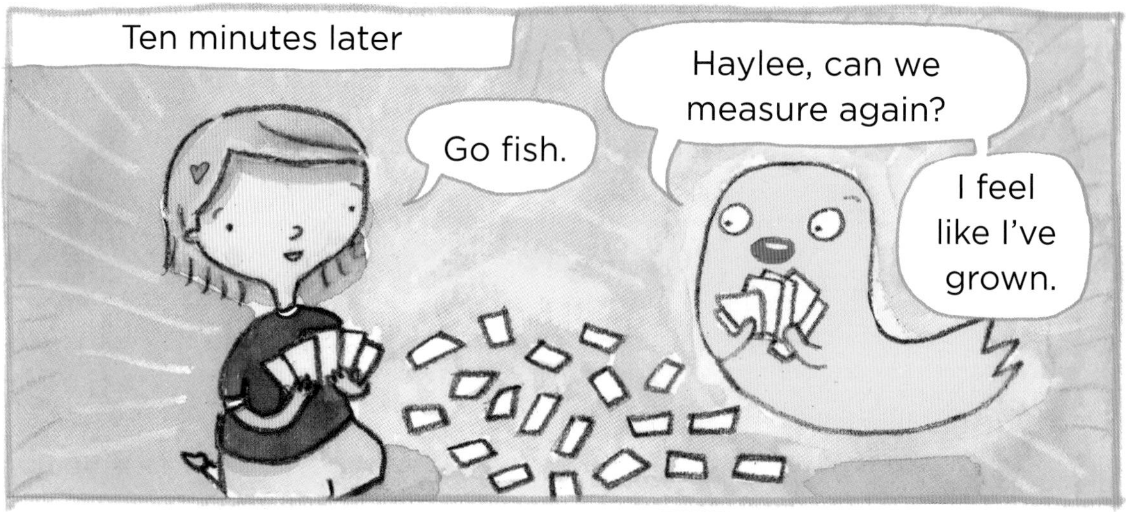
Ten minutes later
Go fish.
Haylee, can we measure again?
I feel like I've grown.

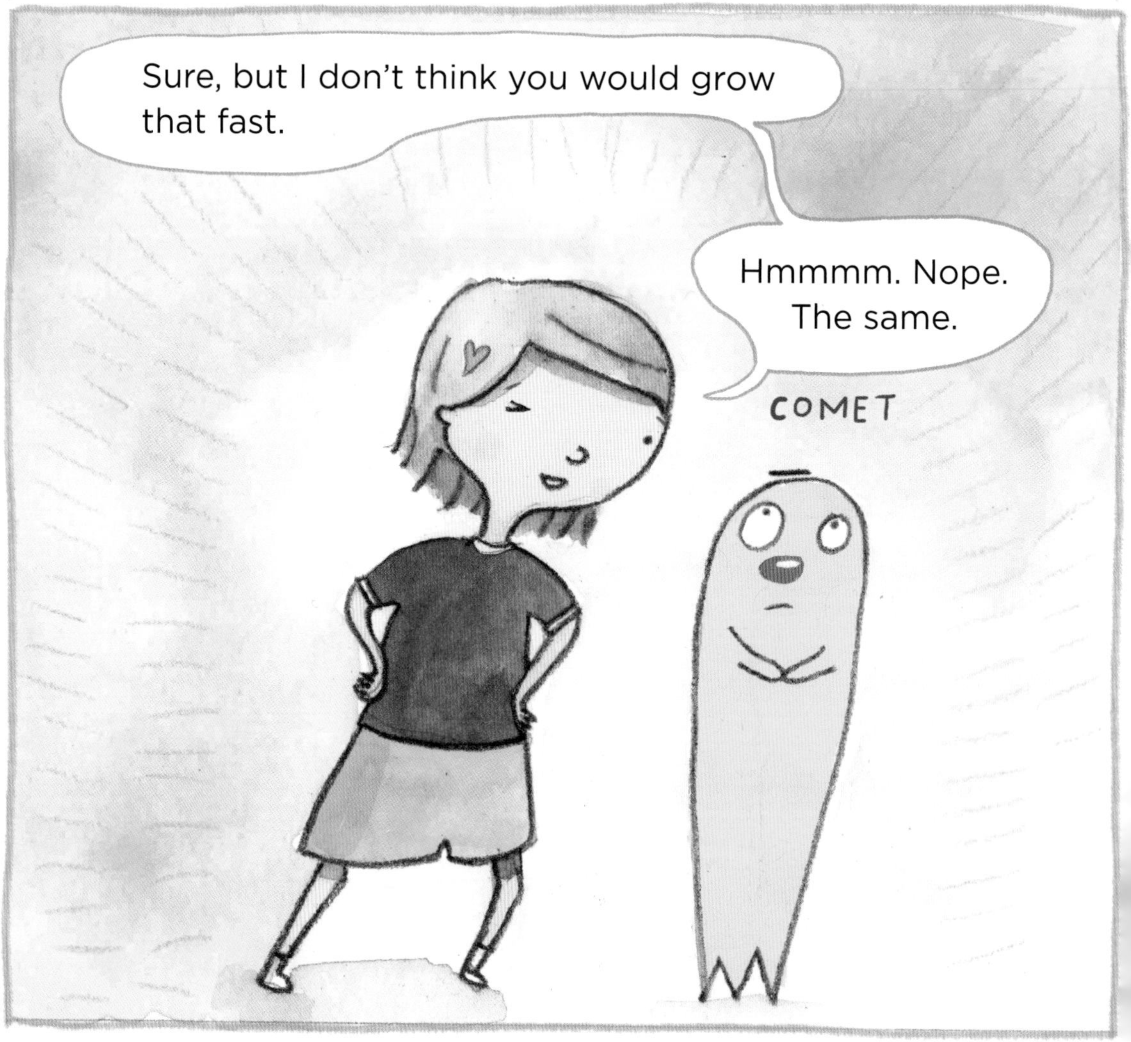
Sure, but I don't think you would grow that fast.
Hmmmm. Nope. The same.
COMET

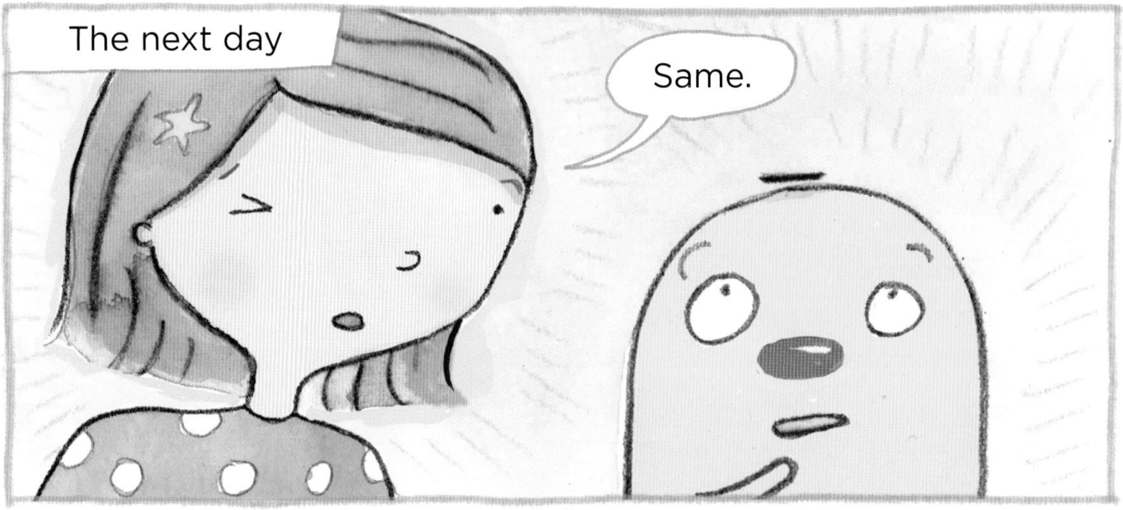
The next day
Same.

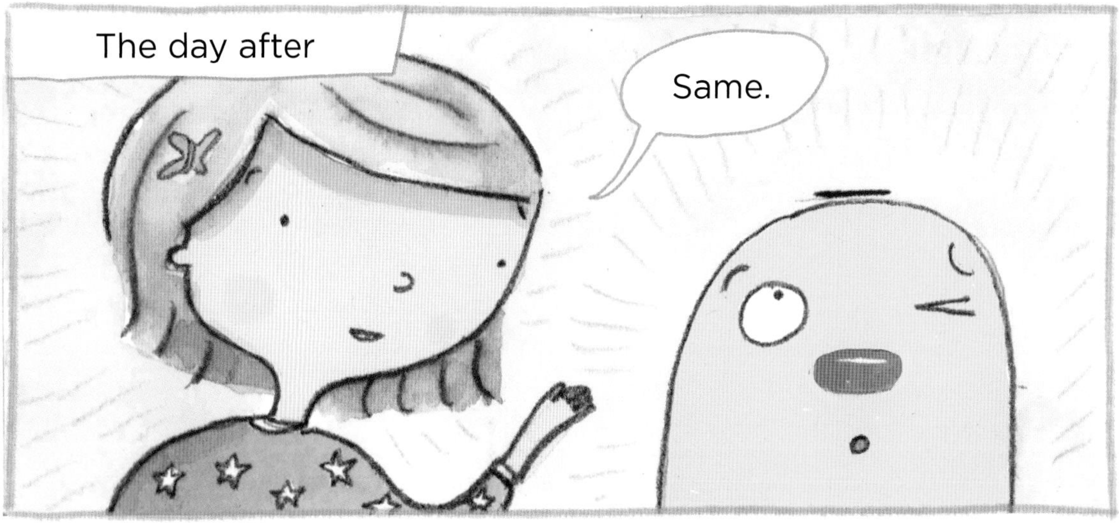
The day after
Same.

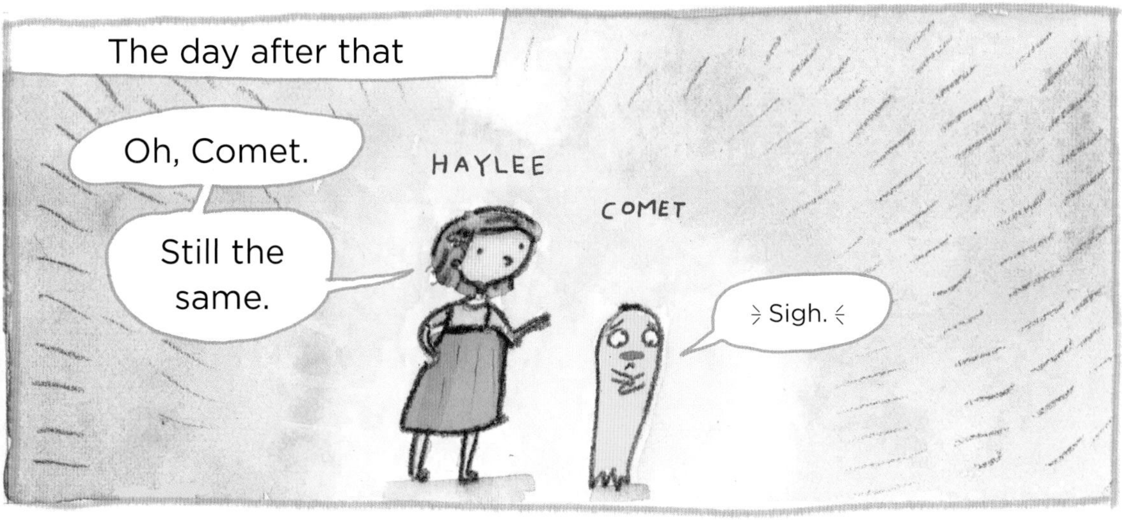
The day after that
Oh, Comet.
Still the same.
HAYLEE
COMET
Sigh.

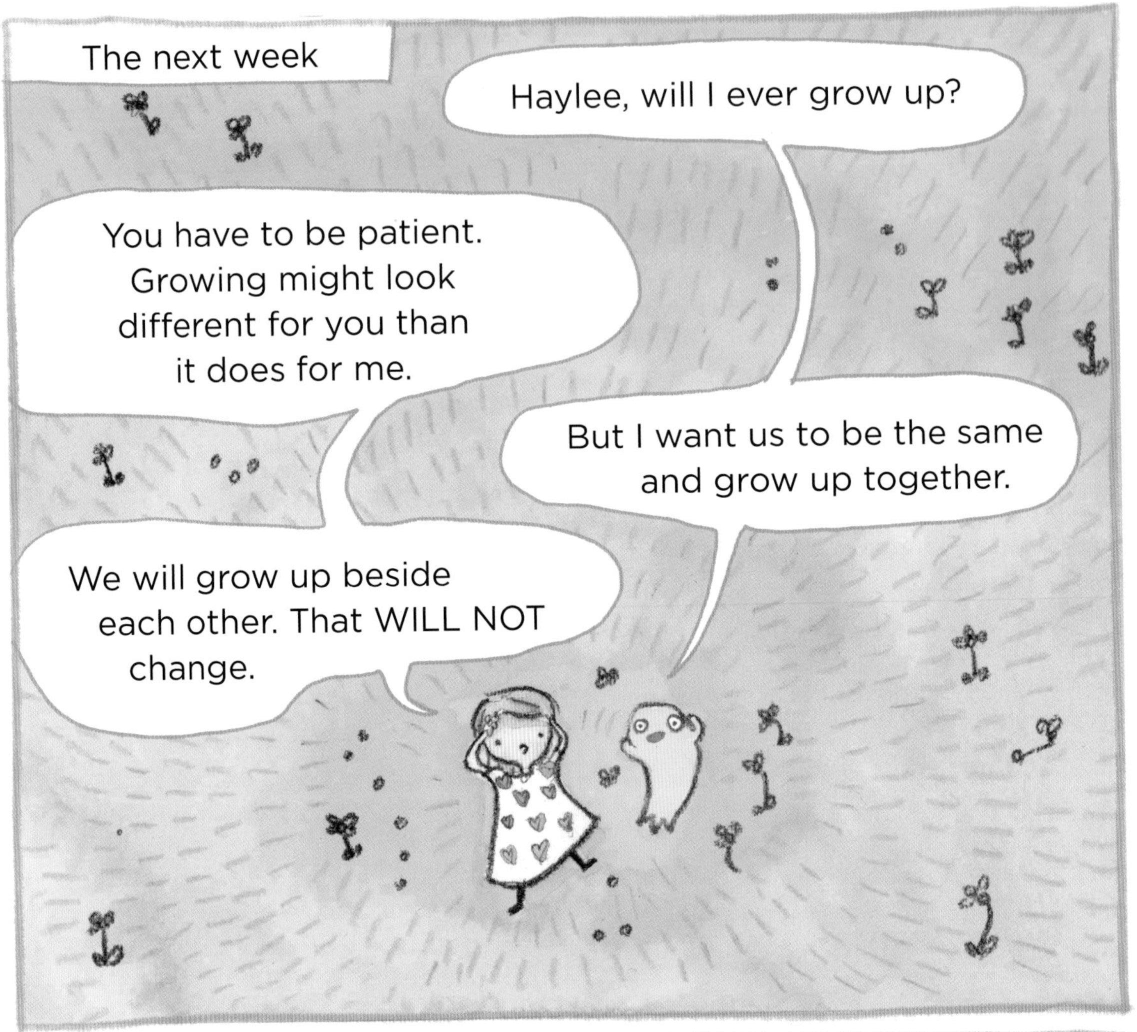
The next week
Haylee, will I ever grow up?
You have to be patient. Growing might look different for you than it does for me.
But I want us to be the same and grow up together.
We will grow up beside each other. That WILL NOT change.

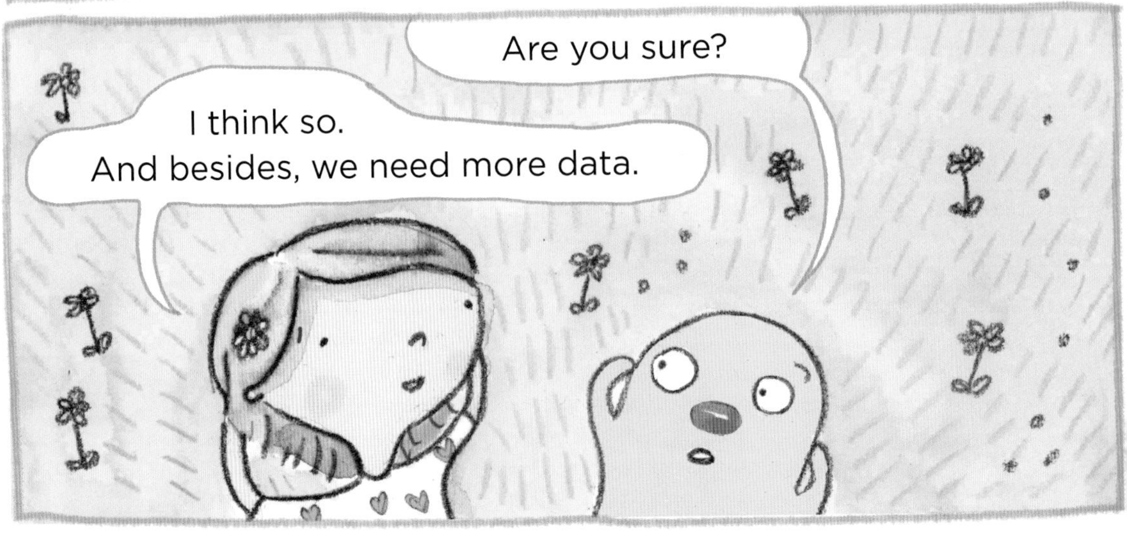
Are you sure?
I think so.
And besides, we need more data.

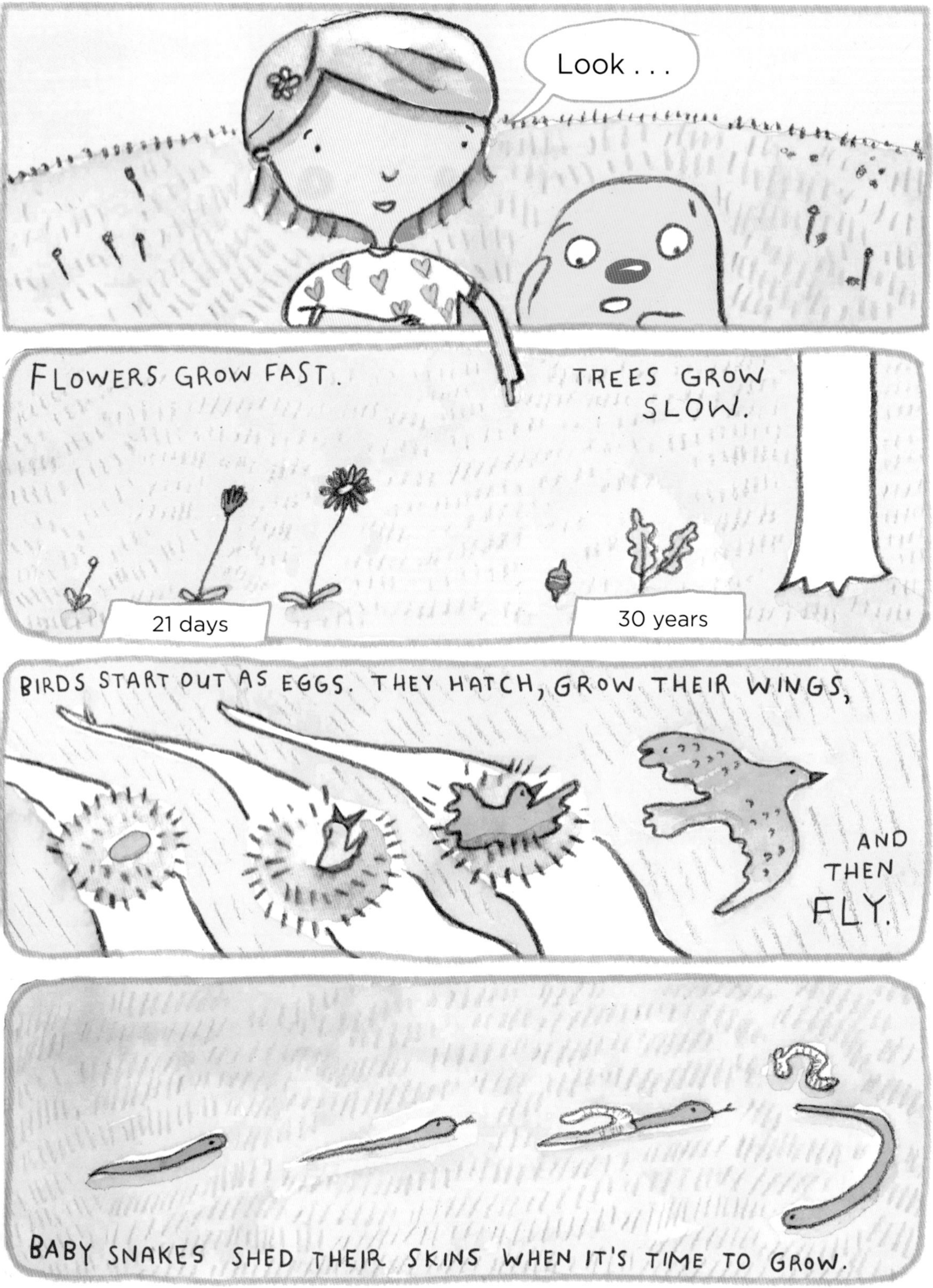
Look . . .
FLOWERS GROW FAST.
TREES GROW SLOW.
21 days
30 years
BIRDS START OUT AS EGGS. THEY HATCH, GROW THEIR WINGS,
AND THEN FLY.
BABY SNAKES SHED THEIR SKINS WHEN IT'S TIME TO GROW.

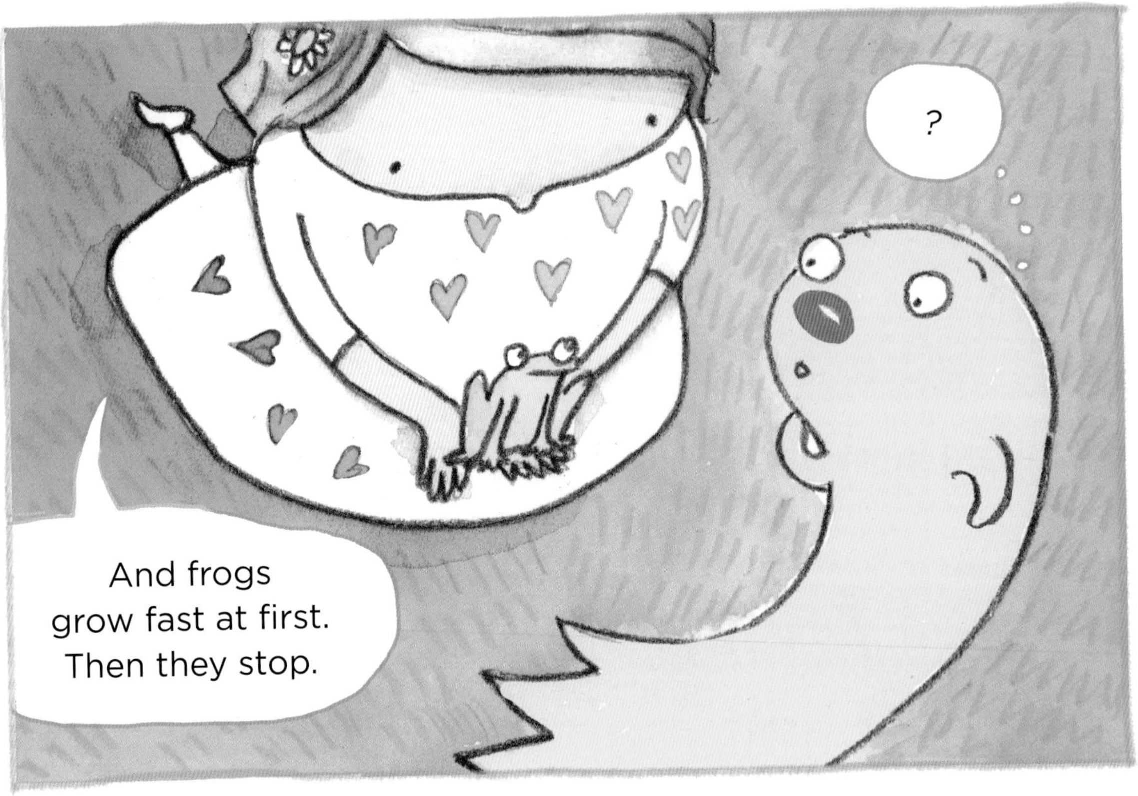
?
And frogs grow fast at first. Then they stop.

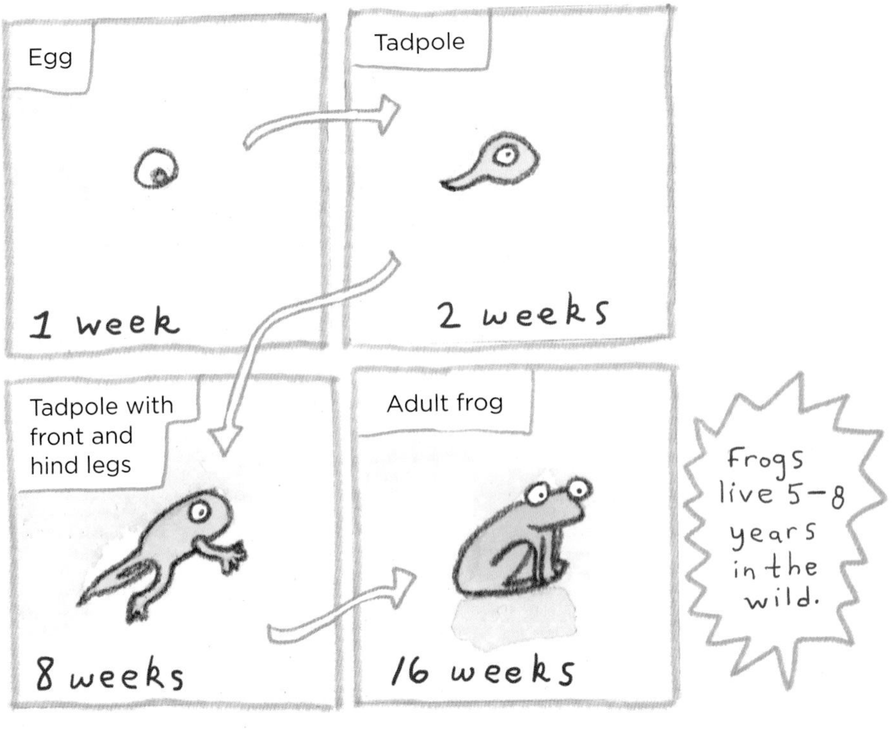
Egg
1 week
Tadpole
2 weeks
Tadpole with front and hind legs
8 weeks
Adult frog
16 weeks
Frogs live 5–8 years in the wild.

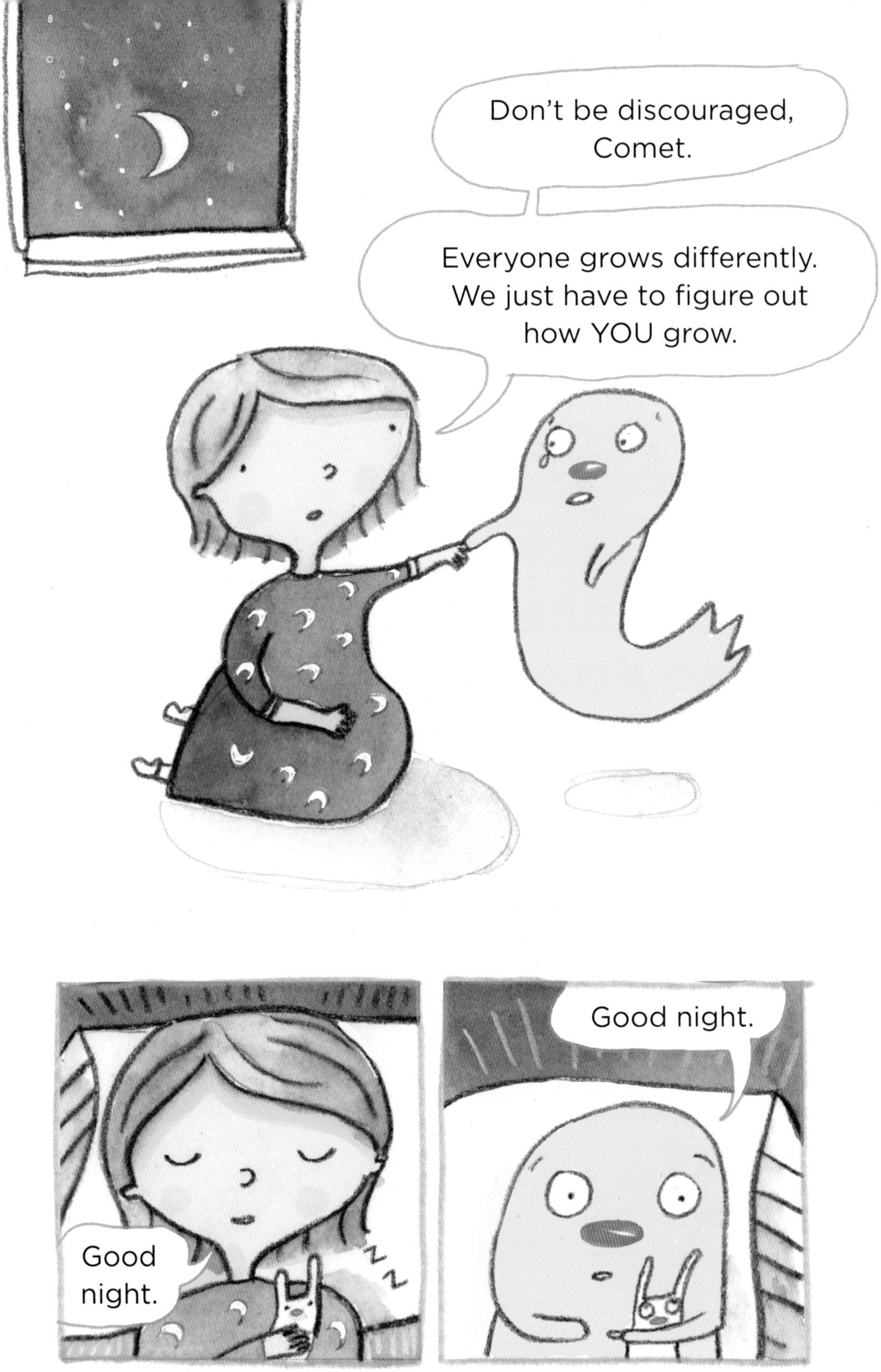
Don't be discouraged, Comet.
Everyone grows differently. We just have to figure out how YOU grow.
Good night.
Good night.

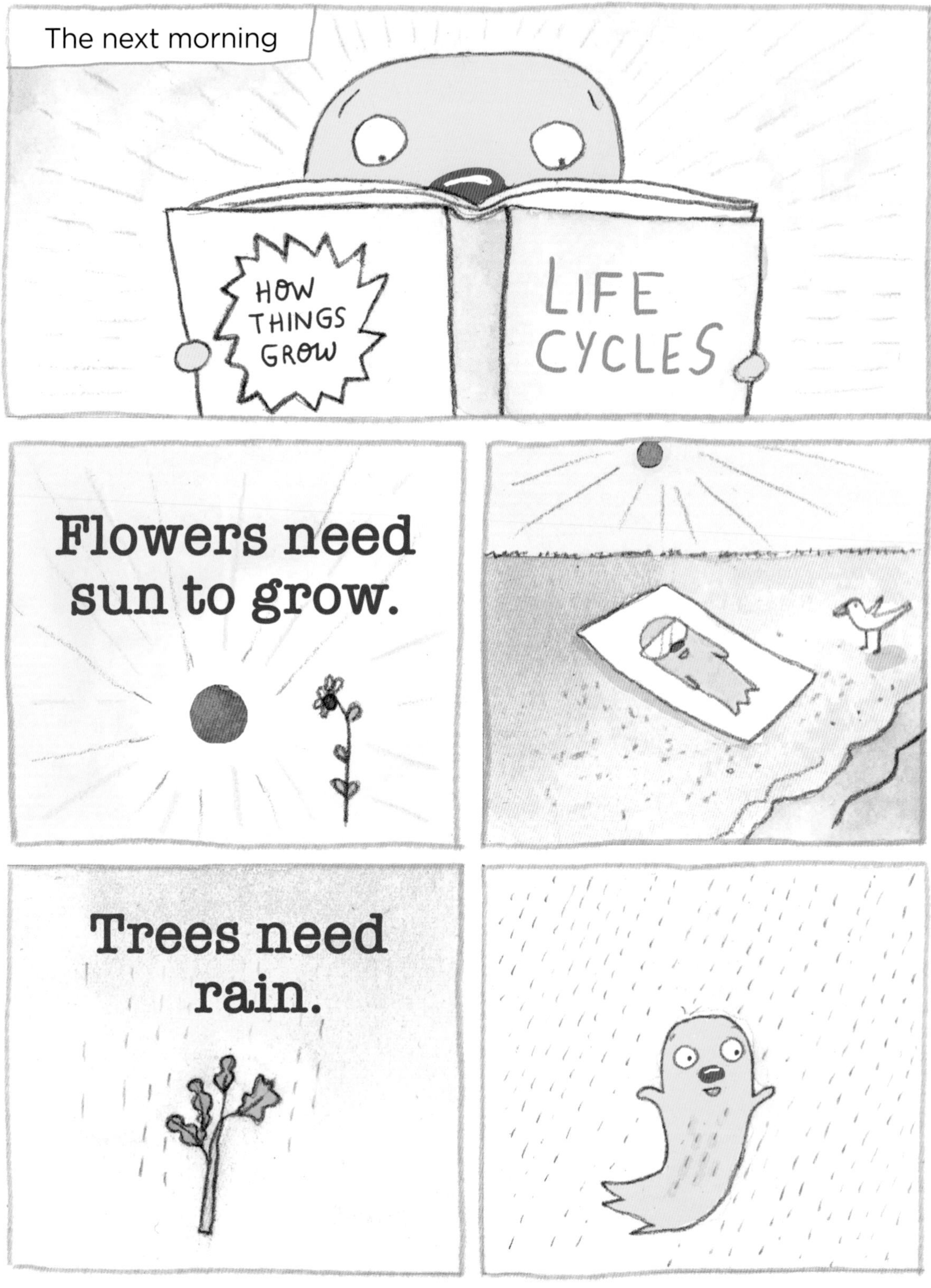
The next morning
HOW THINGS GROW
LIFE CYCLES
Flowers need sun to grow.
Trees need rain.

Bird eggs need mama birds.

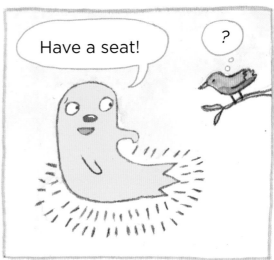

Have a seat!

?

Tadpoles need to eat greens.

Snakes shed skins to grow.

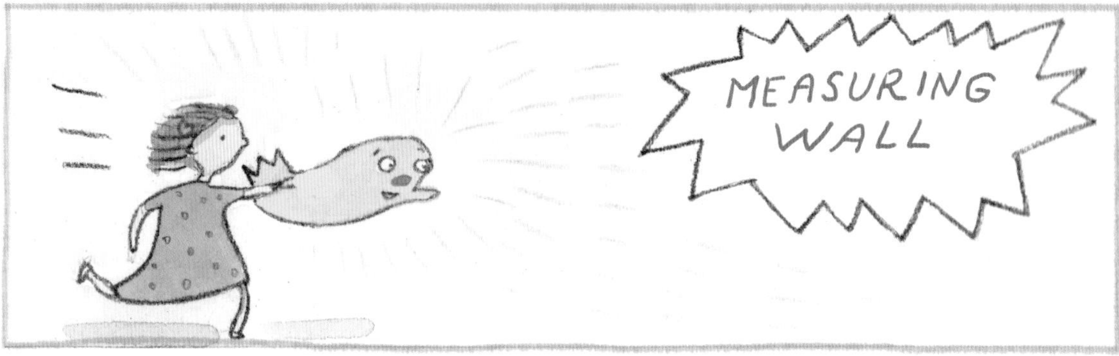
MEASURING WALL

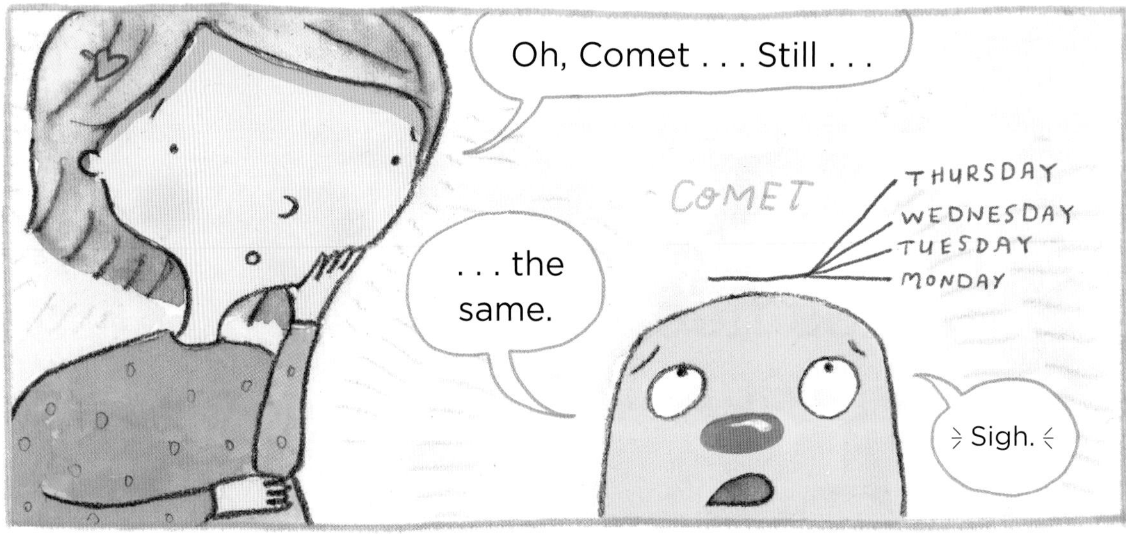
Oh, Comet . . . Still . . .
COMET
THURSDAY
WEDNESDAY
TUESDAY
MONDAY
. . . the same.
Sigh.

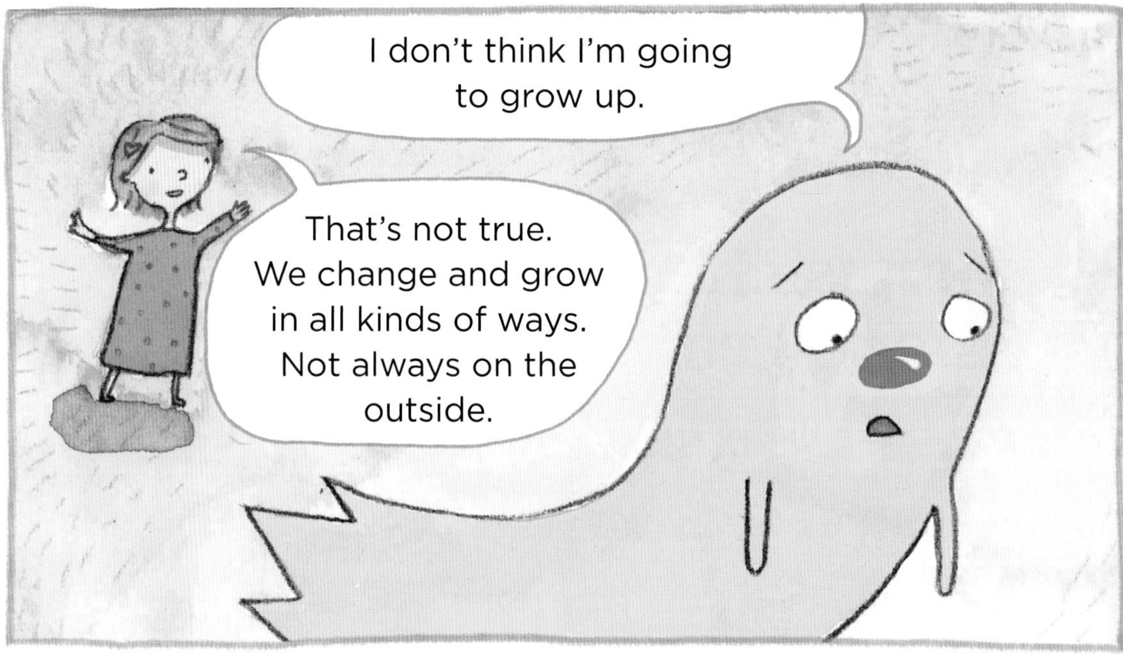
I don't think I'm going to grow up.
That's not true. We change and grow in all kinds of ways. Not always on the outside.

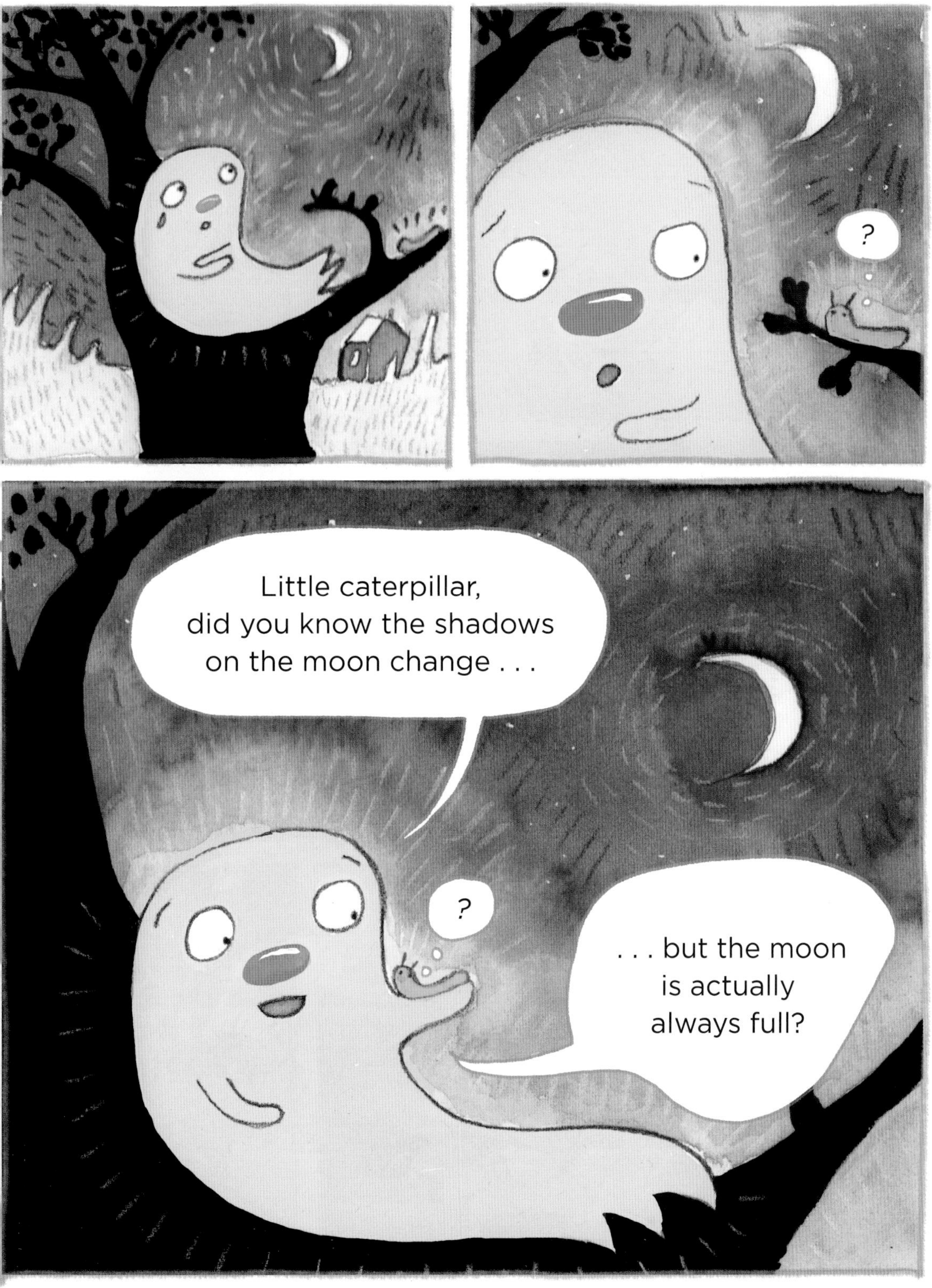
?
Little caterpillar, did you know the shadows on the moon change . . .
?
. . . but the moon is actually always full?

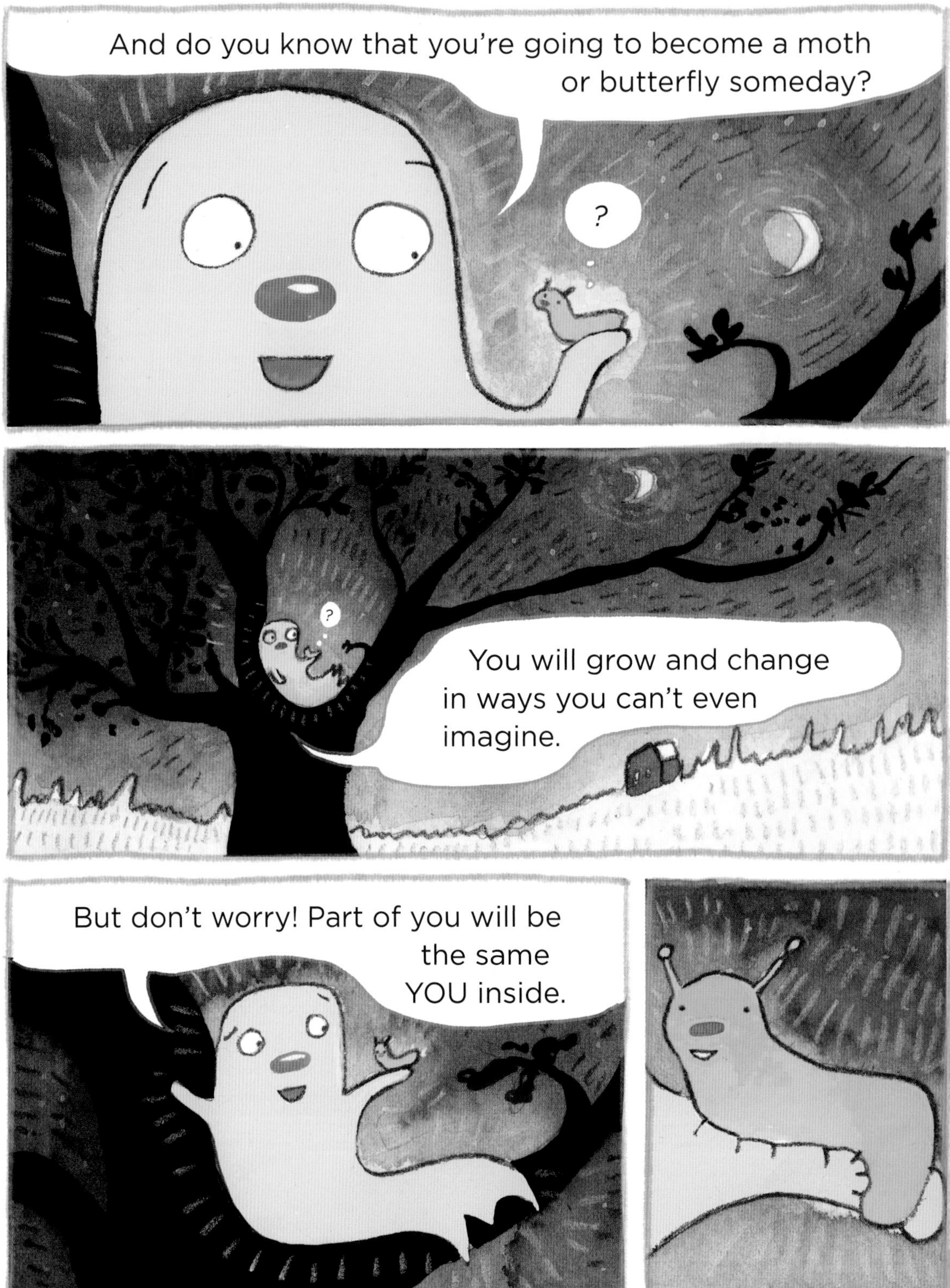
And do you know that you're going to become a moth or butterfly someday?
?
?
You will grow and change in ways you can't even imagine.
But don't worry! Part of you will be the same YOU inside.

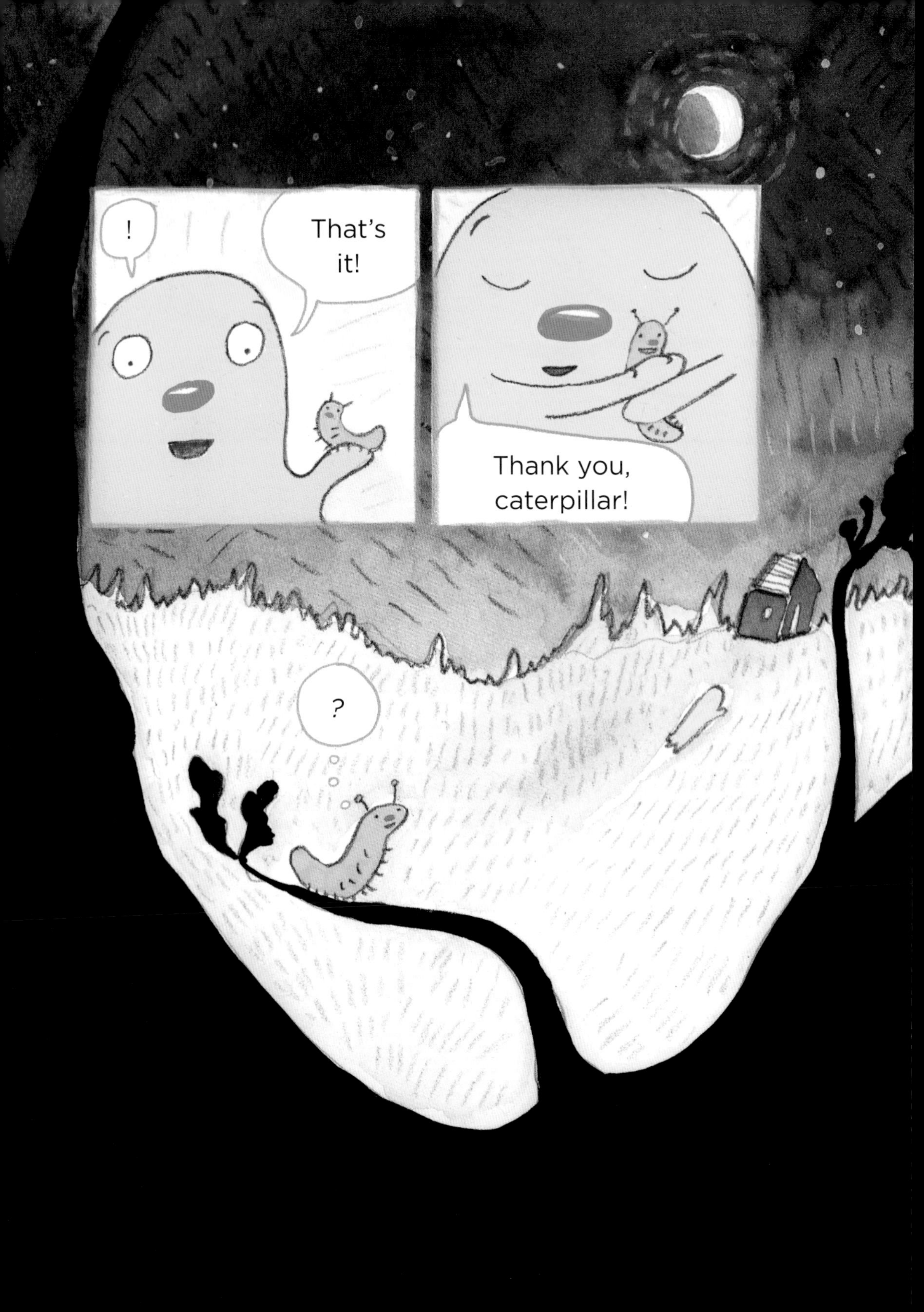
!
That's it!
Thank you, caterpillar!
?

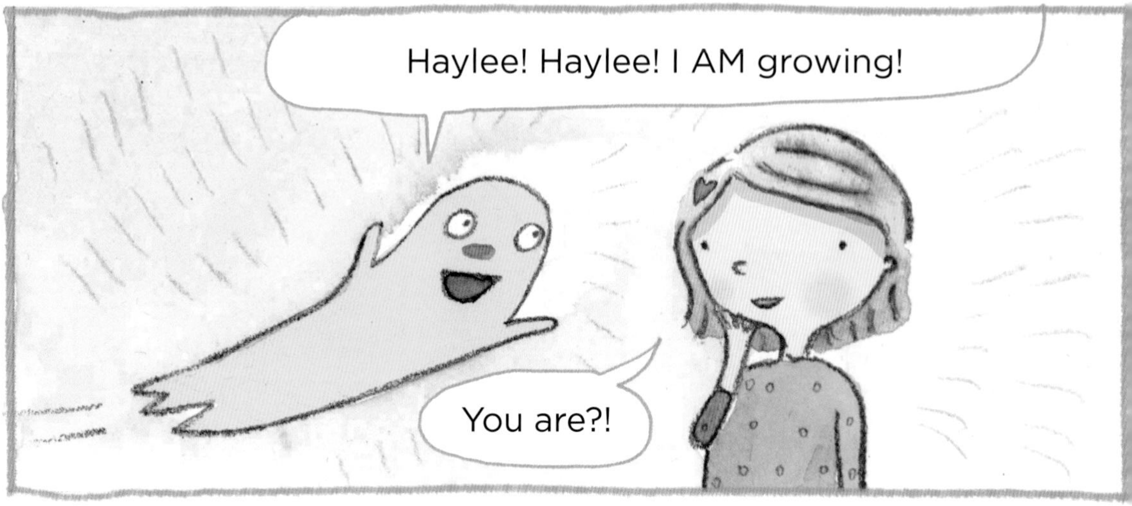
Haylee! Haylee! I AM growing!
You are?!

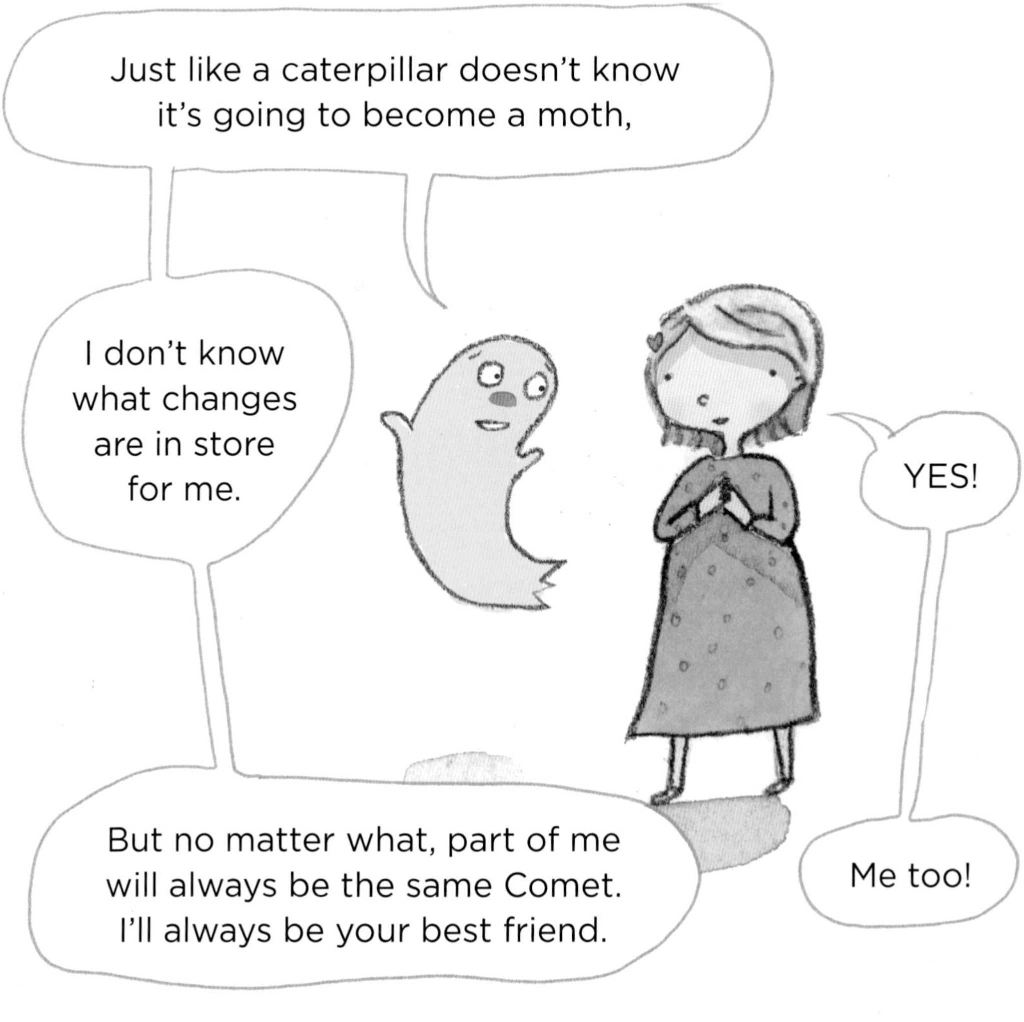
Just like a caterpillar doesn't know it's going to become a moth,
I don't know what changes are in store for me.
YES!
But no matter what, part of me will always be the same Comet. I'll always be your best friend.
Me too!

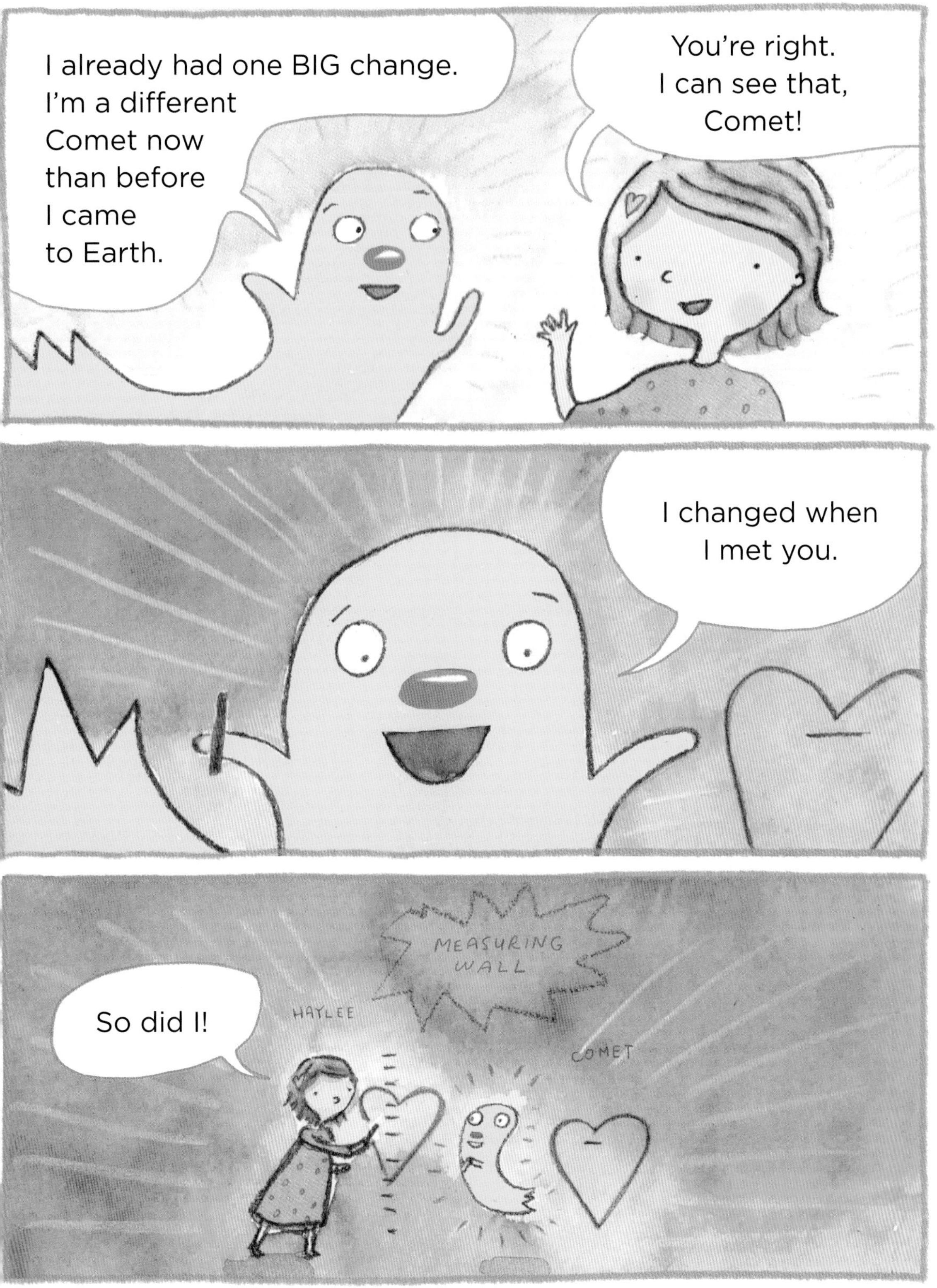
I already had one BIG change. I'm a different Comet now than before I came to Earth.
You're right. I can see that, Comet!
I changed when I met you.
MEASURING WALL
HAYLEE
COMET
So did I!

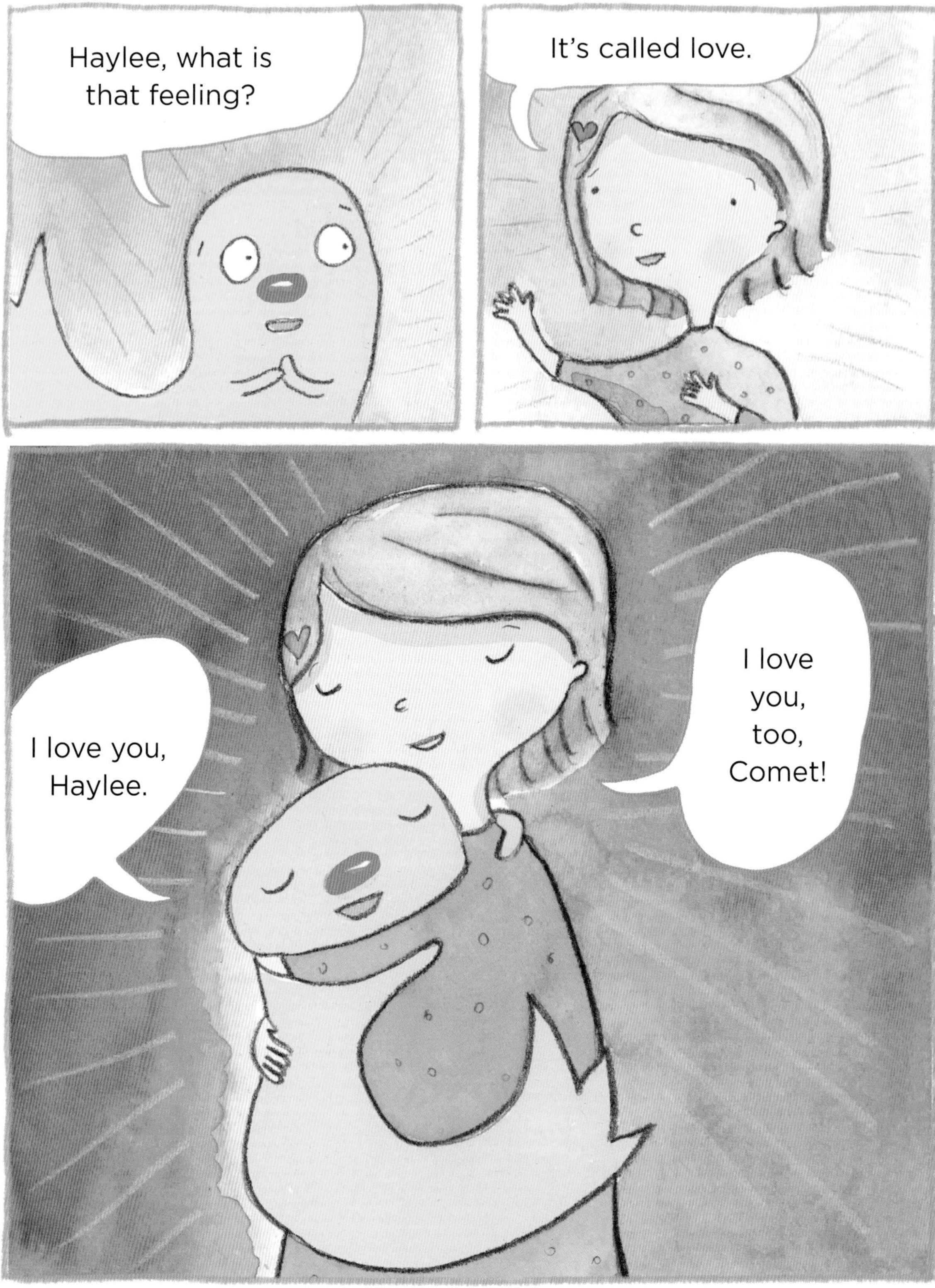
Haylee, what is that feeling?
It's called love.
I love you, Haylee.
I love you, too, Comet!

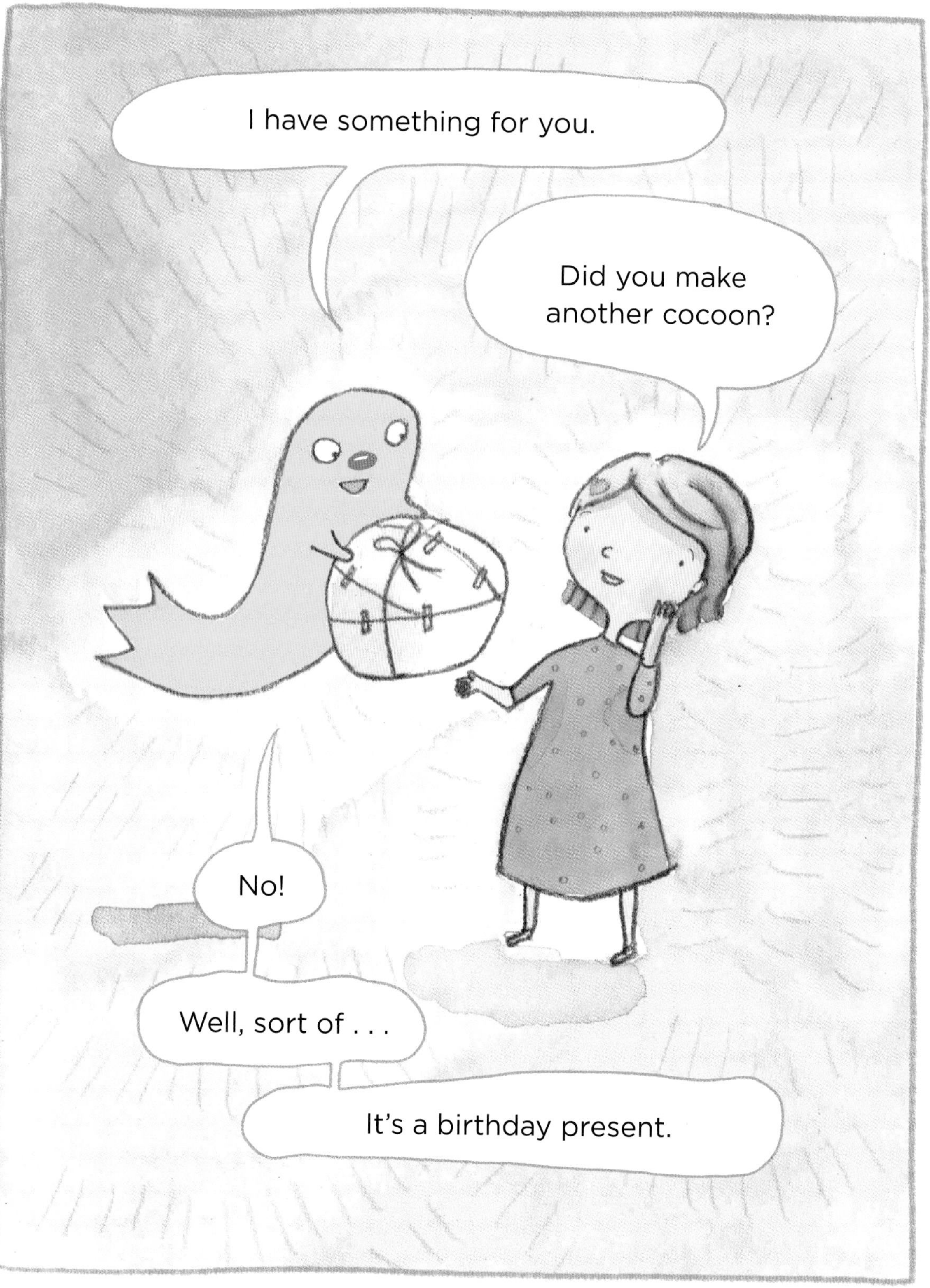
I have something for you.
Did you make another cocoon?
No!
Well, sort of . . .
It's a birthday present.

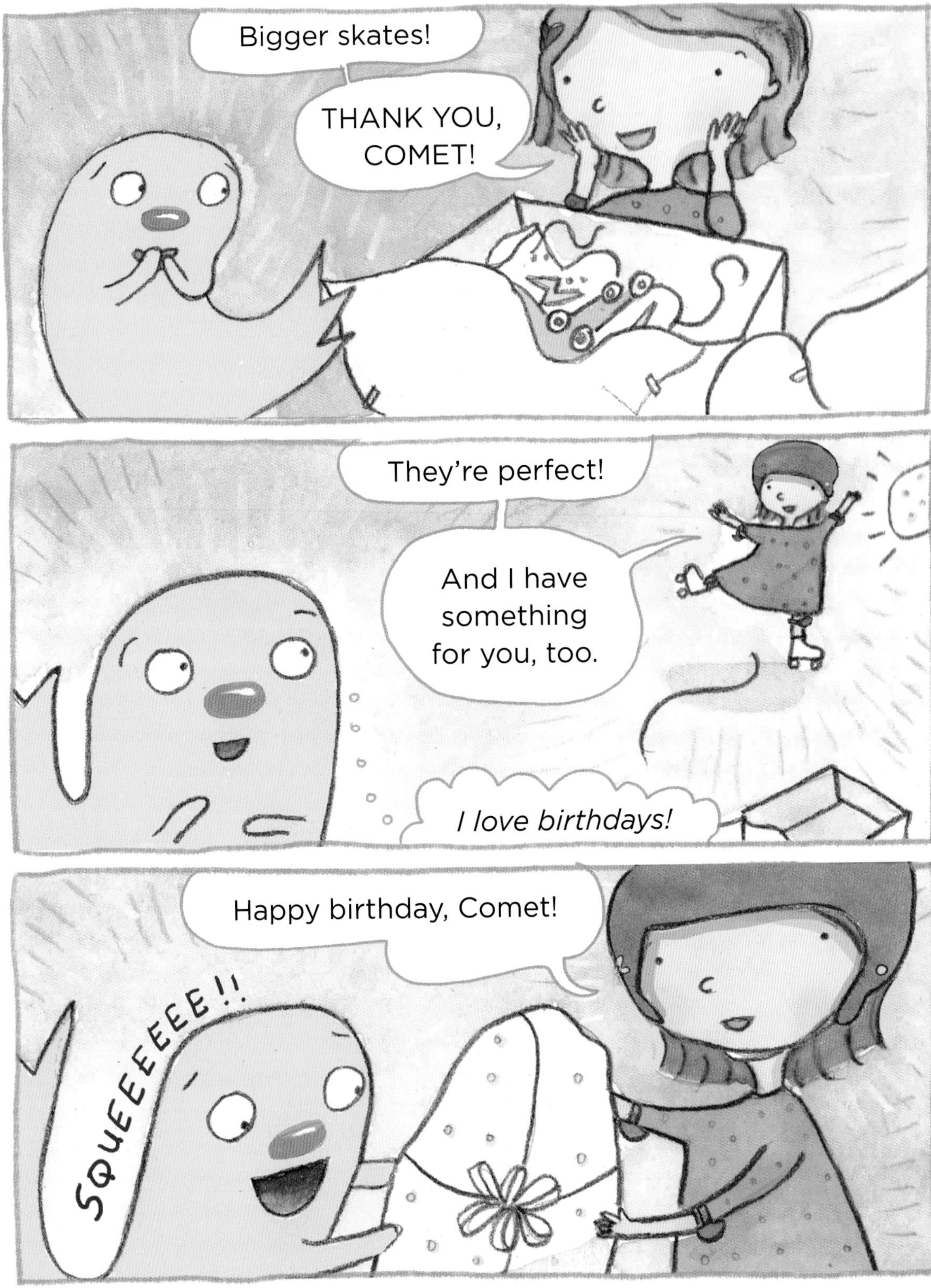
Bigger skates!
THANK YOU, COMET!
They're perfect!
And I have something for you, too.
I love birthdays!
Happy birthday, Comet!
SQUEEEEEEE!!

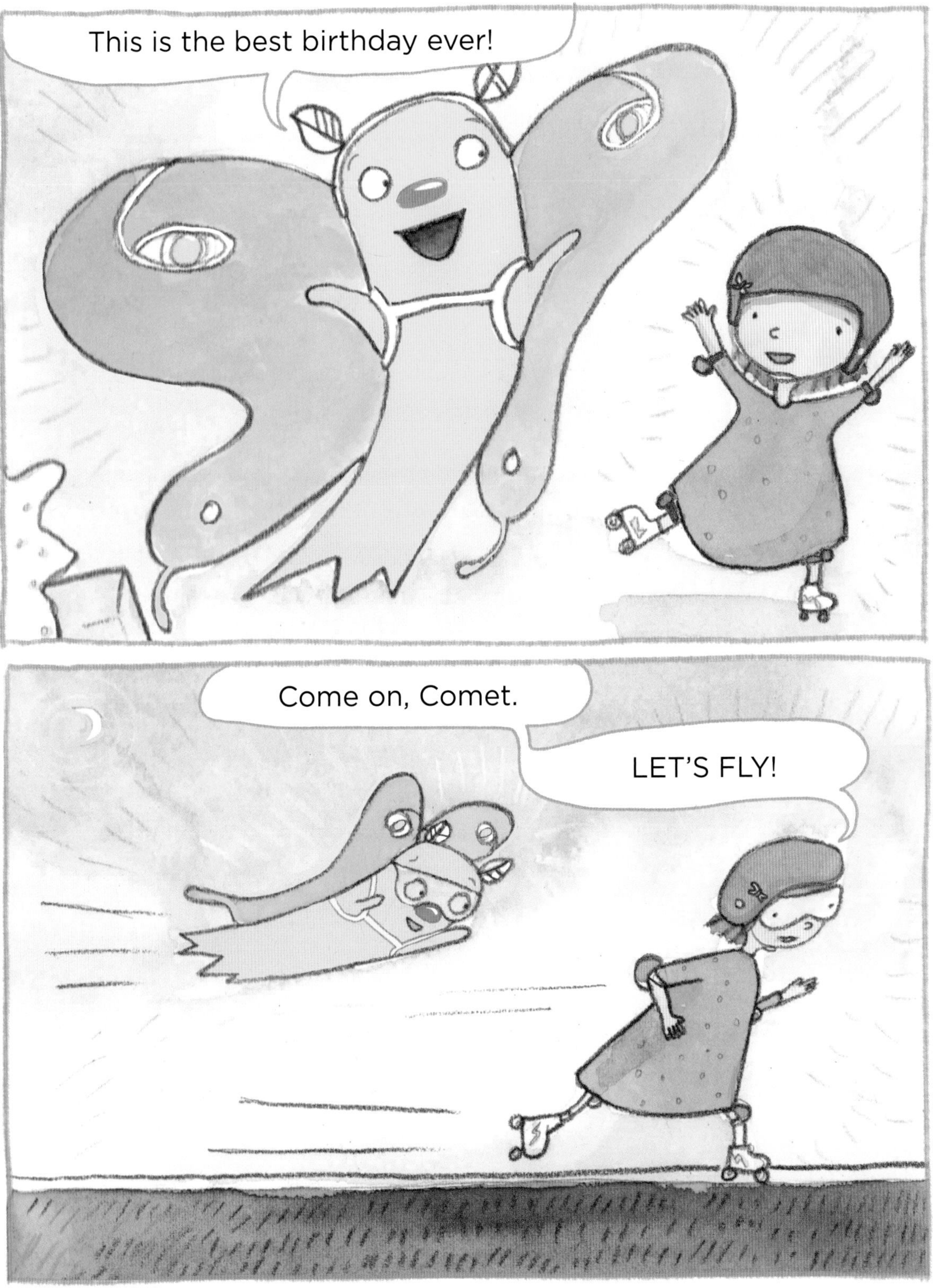
This is the best birthday ever!
Come on, Comet.
LET'S FLY!

EXTRA! EXTRA! HOW OLD ARE YOU?

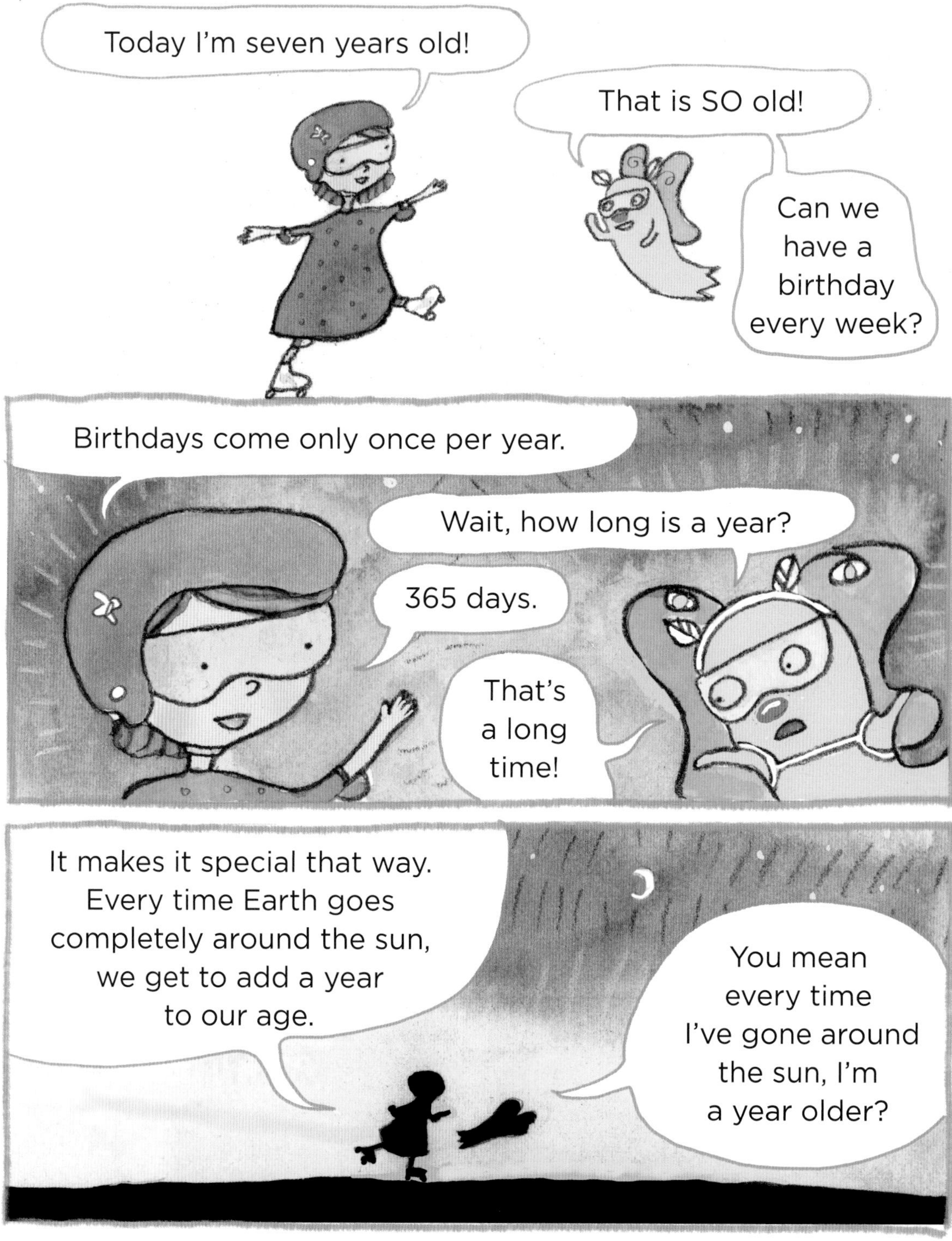
Today I'm seven years old!
That is SO old!
Can we have a birthday every week?
Birthdays come only once per year.
Wait, how long is a year?
365 days.
That's a long time!
It makes it special that way. Every time Earth goes completely around the sun, we get to add a year to our age.
You mean every time I've gone around the sun, I'm a year older?

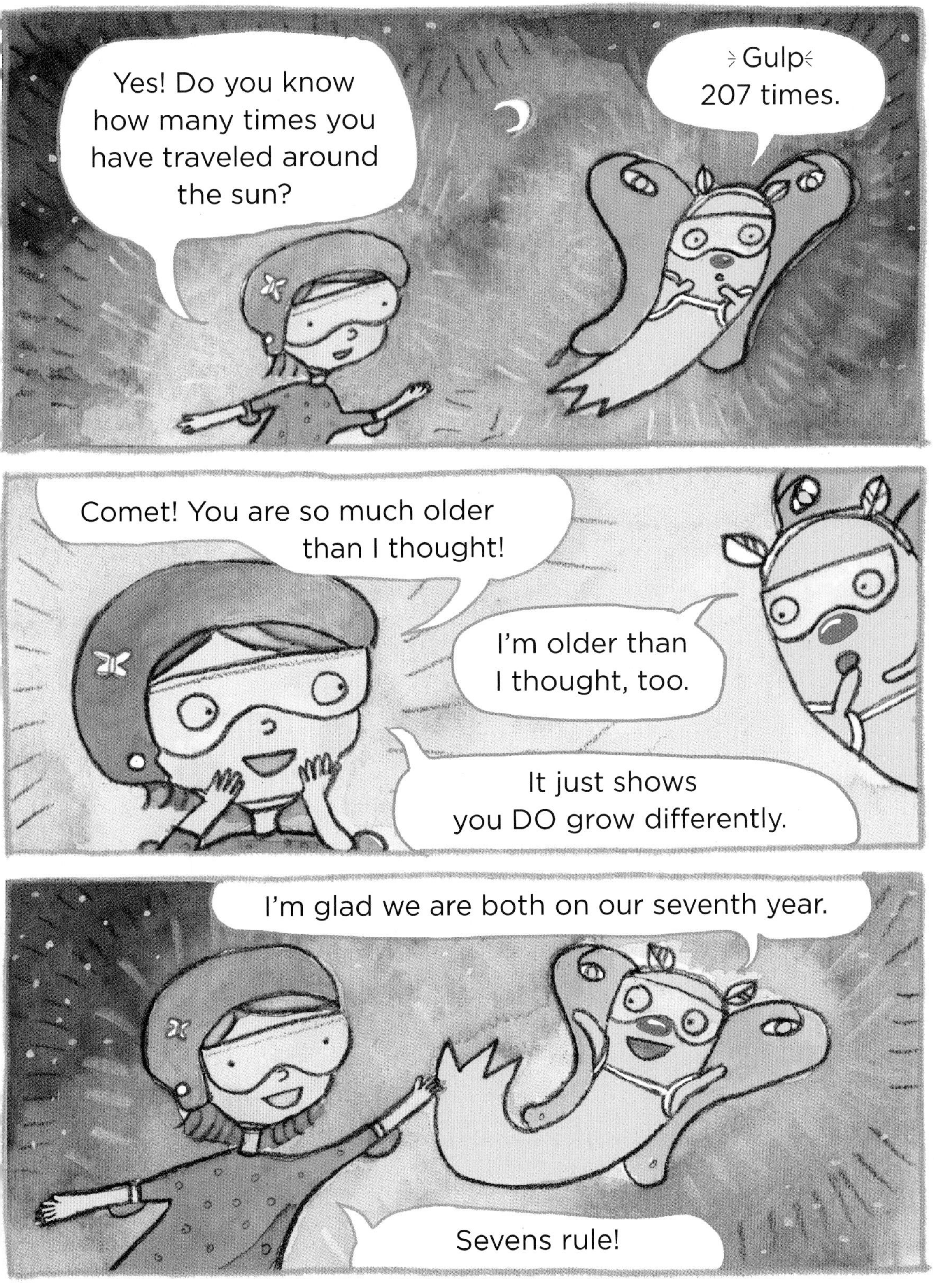
Yes! Do you know how many times you have traveled around the sun?
⋟Gulp⋞
207 times.
Comet! You are so much older than I thought!
I'm older than I thought, too.
It just shows you DO grow differently.
I'm glad we are both on our seventh year.
Sevens rule!

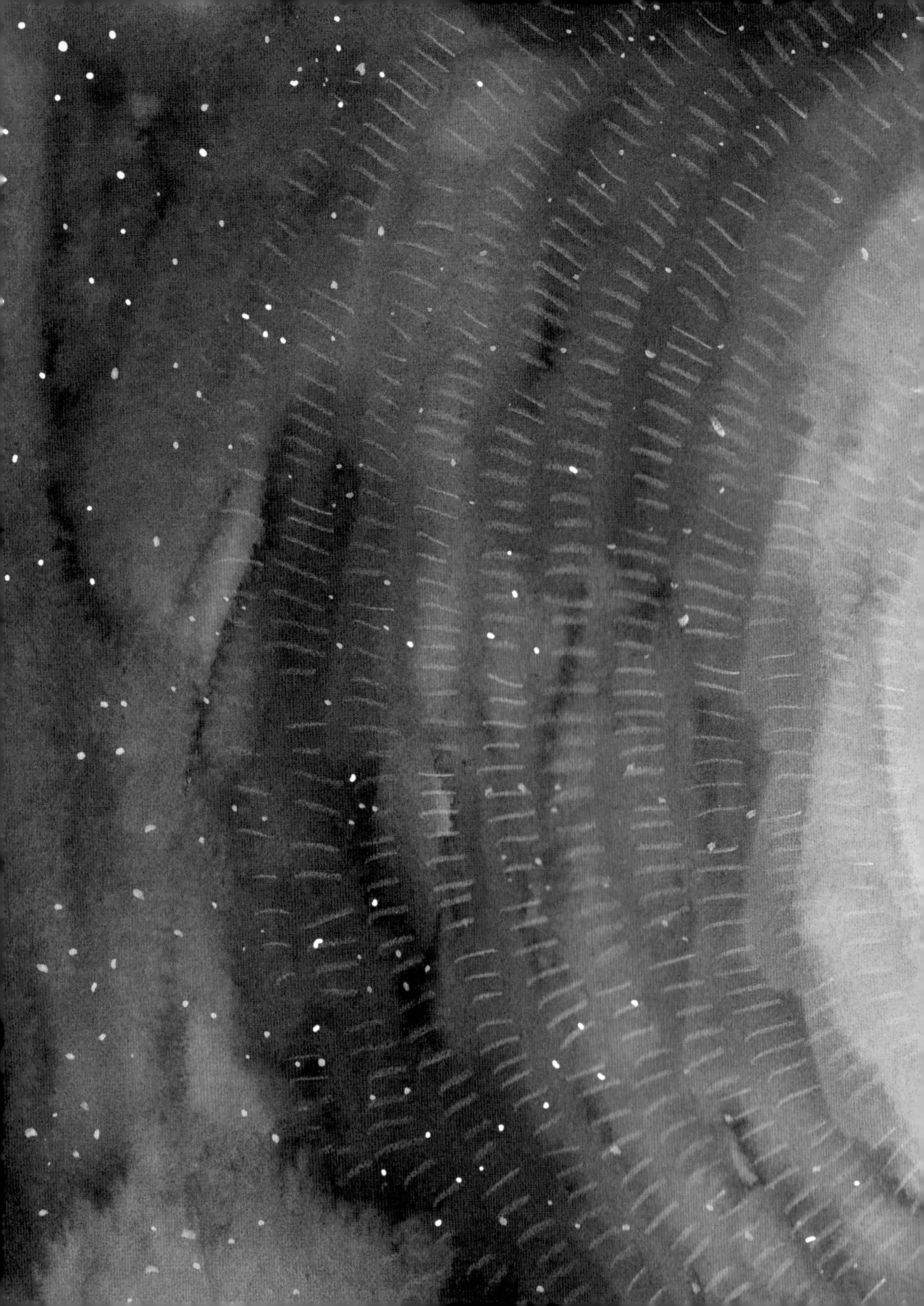